I always knew I had it in me. ~~To kill someone, that is.~~
But killing is the easy part. Getting away with it, on the other hand, that's when it becomes tricky.

However, if you can get past the murder, the crime, the dirty deed, life can become quite interesting.

I'm currently lying by the pool in the surging heat, smoking a cigarette and drinking an ice-cool beer, both courtesy of my friend, presently lying in state in the garage freezer.

I'm waiting for them to come, and they will, but until they do, settle in and I'll tell you my story...

Everyone Smokes
In Paris

A.R. Gill

Published by Conn7 Publishing
Editor: Helena Fairfax
Cover Art © 2023 by Miblart
Published September 2023

ISBN 978-1-7395171-1-3

To my family, especially my wife Danielle,
who never stopped listening to my pipe dream

1

I was standing at the same spot on the platform I'd stood at every weekday for the past eighteen years, in front of the coffee shop selling average flat whites for an exorbitant price. 07:18. Same time, different day. After a while, the morning hustle slowly pushed me to the edge of the platform, way beyond the yellow line that protected us all from a possible death. A slight nudge now at the right time could end all my worries. The debt, the affair, the cancer – all crushed beneath the steel wheels of a passing InterCity.

Same woman, different day. She was sixty, sixty-five, I guess. Cheap perfume and bad skin. Black bobbed hair that wasn't cared for, overweight and wobbled with a stick. She smiled at me and I smiled back.

Same man, different day. Pushing retirement, outstretched arms holding a large newspaper, a maroon trilby that had seen better days and that never, ever matched his scruffy attire. He smelled of Perique and

Pure Virginia tobacco. I knew the blend as it was one my late grandfather smoked constantly, from an old briar pipe that was now in my possession.

Same people, different day. The couple, late fifties, who were still very much in love, constantly kissing between giggling whispers; the teenage boy with the loud, aggressive music blaring from an iPhone, out of bulky headphones; the tall, wiry, thirty-something guy, with black, oversized, square-rimmed glasses, dark-haired, and handsome. Clark Kent, eat your heart out. The petite and immaculate middle-aged lady, Burberry mac and red heels, a small, fancy dog wedged between her arm and a slim waistline.

I peered down the track, the rails fading away into the glum January morning. It was cold and damp.

The 07:26 chugged into the station at 07:31, full-beam headlights cutting through the darkness of a different day, its slow approach alerting an impatient public, who were shuffling their feet as they altered their positions.

The same woman, but on a different day, edged closer to me. I could smell the tea she'd drunk that morning; I could see the cavities in her mouth as a crooked smile developed into a yawn; I could feel her warm breath against my beard.

The beard was a new thing. It was unkempt, more laziness than fashion, and my hair had grown long and had no real style. I'd been told in the past I was a handsome man, with soulful eyes and a good smile. But that was the past and today was today.

The door to the coach hissed open, and the usual pushing and shoving followed. I stepped on board and found a vacant seat in the corner, next to a window dripping with condensation. The warmth inside was welcoming; it felt good to feel my fingers and thumbs again. I peered around the carriage. Same Monday-morning zombie express containing the living dead, all of them distraught another weekend had passed so quickly.

The doors shut with the same hiss they'd opened with. I closed my eyes and thought of Penny. I thought of the debt she was yet to know about. Christ, she'd already supported me through the cancer, forgiven me for the affair – well, the one she knew about, at least. I still had the other bitch threatening me.

Continue or I tell Penny today was the text I'd woken to this morning. Ursula. This one had been trouble from the start. A real bunny boiler. Three cheap fucks in a budget hotel and she'd declared her love to me, said she'd leave her husband. Goddam it, she had three young girls, all under the age of five. How could she say it, let alone go through with it?

She was nothing like her sister. The complete

9

opposite, in fact. Penny.

Fuck, my dear Penny. How much more could she take? She deserved better. So much better. Someone to worship the ground she walked on and not someone who just trampled all over her.

Monday morning would always be a fresh start, a new me, a new life. That was until one o'clock came along and the first line was snorted. Oh yeah, that was another thing…

The train jolted, breaking me from my thoughts. I opened my eyes. My fellow passenger in the adjacent seat was an elderly woman, all bones. She was reading a thick book, the pages yellow with age. The print was small, but her bifocals would help. I couldn't see the title, but I was sure it was something I would never have read. The seat opposite me was empty, and next to that sat a rangy, middle-aged guy. He had his eyes shut, arms folded. He had thinning ginger hair swept across a greasy forehead, and a drinker's nose, red and bumpy. His clothes were old and covered in grime, and his steel-capped boots were covered in dust. There was a robust-looking yellow bucket wedged between his legs, filled with tools spilling to the brim. He was listening to music through clunky headphones, the type with the radio built in. They looked cheap; I could hear every line to a blues song.

I closed my eyes again and thought back to Penny, how it was before the shit, before the fog, and slipped into a dream, a better place. I wouldn't wake until I reached my final destination. Only thirty minutes to go.

2

I was woken by a chorus of announcements and a chill I felt right the way through to my spine. Through lazy eyes I saw the carriage was now empty, the hustle and bustle replaced by a scattering of redundant newspapers. I stood up reluctantly. I could have slept for a whole week. Maybe even two.

I headed towards the open doors. Final destination – Monday morning ready to slap me right across the face again. The cold air outside awaited me – January, bleak and dull.

I made my way with apprehensive steps and my head in a whirl, my body in the present and my mind elsewhere. I was downbeat, lacking energy, a fucking mess.

I glanced up at a poster above the exit as I stepped off the carriage. 'Cyprus' written in bold letters, the perfect family frolicking on a golden beach under a tranquil sun. I envisaged it for a second: Penny and I strolling hand-in-hand along an endless shoreline, the squidgy sand between our toes, the subtle sound of gentle waves echoing into a perfect horizon. If only.

I pulled myself out of the poster and glanced down. Something caught my attention, glistening on the floor beneath me. A metal object, no more than six inches long. I picked it up.

It was a Stanley knife. The blade was retracted into the casing. I released it. The brittle blade seemed new. I imagined it in the wrong hands, not mine, and put it in my suit jacket pocket. I would hand it in to one of the staff at the station. The rangy guy must have let if fall out of his bucket, oblivious, mesmerised by the mournful music of the Deep South. It had also been missed by everyone else. The rat race, a zombie apocalypse moving out, no care, no time.

I got off the train. Platform 8. Everyone had all but disappeared through the electronic gates into the undesirable future of a working week. I followed hesitantly, my head down, the world on my shoulders, approaching the exit like the last of the human race.

The old lady with the book was still on the platform, just before the row of barriers, on her hands and knees, rummaging in a big bag that looked like it contained the contents of her life. I asked if she was OK.

'I seem to have misplaced my ticket,' she said. She

was flustered.

'Let me check for you.'

She stood up and passed me the bag, looking even more fragile than I remembered. Bones dusted with flesh.

The bag was heavy even for me. Jesus. It must have been a struggle for her – a daily workout. I took a look inside. It contained everything. Old black-and-white photos of a time she probably cherished, bundles of unopened letters, cigarettes (a brand I didn't recognise), several glasses cases that felt empty, scattered make-up, the book (this time I saw the title – I was right I had never read it), crumpled-up tissues, an old mobile phone from before the technology had got stupid, cough sweets, loose change (although not much), a neat leather purse which I asked if I could open. She agreed, so I did. Inside were many train tickets, but none for today. Some cash, maybe fifty pounds, rolled tight. Could have been more. A lipstick, crimson. Nothing else.

I handed the bag back. 'Come with me,' I said.

She followed slowly, the bag a burden. We ambled towards the guard, who looked to be in his sixties, and in his last job. He was wearing a crisp white shirt with a red tie, a big overcoat with the rail company's logo on it, and a peaked cap. The hair visible was grey and neatly cut. He was wide as well as tall. I had to look up at him to speak.

'Excuse me, this lady seems to have misplaced her ticket. Would it be OK to let her through?'

'She'll need to produce a valid ticket.'

'Surely you can just let her through? She's hardly your average fare dodger, is she?'

We both glanced over to where the old lady was standing. She seemed even frailer. A shrinking violet.

'If she can't produce a valid ticket, I will have to charge her for the full fare. Where did you travel from today, my love?'

I interrupted. 'You're fucking kidding me, right?'

'I'm not here to kid, sir. Do I look like a kidder? And please don't talk to me using such language.' He pointed to a poster, something about not abusing staff. Whatever. He was speaking down to me, as though the uniform made him better than me. As though I were a mere schmuck. I began to get angry. Fuck, here we go again. My palms felt clammy, and my heart was pounding.

The antidepressants, among other things, were meant to have a calming effect, suppressing the rage within me. You name it, I was either on it or had tried it. Prozac, Celexa, Zoloft, Luvox, Cipralex. I rattled when I walked, but despite my daily morning ritual popping pills, I never felt any different.

I knew the reason for this. Of course I did. The doctor had made it clear I needed to cut back on the booze – but had I? Had I fuck. I was knocking back three bottles of wine a day, sometimes a bottle of vodka on top of that, sometimes a bottle of whisky on top of that, sometimes...

'She has a bundle of tickets in that bag. She clearly always pays for her travel, she's just misplaced today's. Easily done. Surely it's not going to fucking affect your day in any shape or form to just let her through your fucking precious gate?'

My voice had risen a few decibels. I was definitely shouting now, just like the guy in the poster.

'Without a valid ticket, as I said, she will have to pay the full fare. Now I suggest you get on with your day, sir, and let me deal with the lady directly, before I call security.'

'Security? Fucking security?' Shouting. Guy in the poster. 'I didn't jump the barrier with a load of Semtex strapped around me!'

I turned back at the old lady. She moved closer, smiled and thanked me for my help, but said she was quite happy to pay the fine.

'Are you sure?'

'Quite sure, my love.'

I said goodbye, short and sweet. Quite unusual for a train station platform – no tears, no hugs, no brief encounter.

I inserted my ticket into the machine and the gate

opened. I went through and then looked back over my shoulder, making eye contact with the guard as I did so. He didn't say anything, but gave a sly grin.

You may have won the battle, my friend, but over my dead fucking body are you winning the war.

His time would come. It would, wouldn't it?

I had a seven-minute walk to my office. My habit was to stop and get my usual flat white, with the extra shot, from an independent coffee house I had used for years, which was just outside the station. I would then walk the remaining five-and-a-half minutes to the office, smoking a cigarette that would be my fourth of the day.

The coffee house was mobbed as the rat race got their morning fix. I joined the queue. The interior was trendy, with red brick walls covered with old movie posters. There was one that always caught my attention: *Attack of the 50 Foot Woman*. I had never seen it, had no real intention of seeing it, but it was a great poster, though. An illustration, like most old movie posters. A giant, slim young woman in a white bikini, straddled an overpass, holding a smoking car in her left hand like it was a toy, while reaching down for another. Several cars had crashed below her, and people were crawling away like insects. The colours were great – the title in red, the background and skyline in a bold yellow. I wondered if the film was as good as it appeared.

I edged down the queue until there were three people in front of me. A tall black guy in a grey overcoat was being served. He bought a Diet Coke, no coffee. What a waste of space. The music they played was loud, and always something funky and hip – usually something I didn't recognise but I always tapped my foot to it. Today was different – a psychedelic soul number I did recognise. I mouthed the words. I knew every line.

I finally got served and paid for my stimulant with a twenty. The same twenty I'd sniffed coke from last night; the same coke that made me feel great at the time and shit right now. I thought about the day ahead and how I was going to get through. I would have called in sick, but I was on my final written warning. Another missed Monday and they would send me packing.

The guy serving me messed about in the till, collecting my change.

'No five-pound notes, I'm afraid,' he said, in a foreign accent.

'OK,' I said, begrudgingly.

I slipped my hand into my pocket to see if I had the correct change, save the twenty to snort a rotund line of powder later – the highlight and then the downfall of my day.

I rummaged around. No change, just my passport. I was supposedly meeting a loan shark tonight.

'Supposedly' because I couldn't believe it had come to this. My dealer had put me onto this guy – two grand at an excruciating interest and your passport as security. Rob Peter to pay Paul. Good business for everyone, apart from me.

As well as the passport there was something else, unexpected. Shit.

The roll of notes from the old lady's purse. I must have put it in my pocket by mistake. I'd become a lot of things of late, but someone who steals from a pensioner was not going to be one of them. The lowest of the low, crackheads with no shame about where their next hit was coming from. I wasn't there yet. Hopefully I never would be. Hopefully.

I left the guy behind the counter holding a fistful of coins and a steaming hot flat white and ran out of the shop, bumping into several people I didn't make eye contact with. They were pissed off. I didn't apologise.

I was back at platform 8 and out of breath, my lungs burning, my heart pounding. Thirty-a-day habit right here and now.

I was just in time. The old lady had passed through the barrier and was standing in the middle of the concourse looking up at the departure board, searching for her next destination. The guard was still on the other side of the barrier, a blur in the background, only his overwhelming size distinguishing him from the other guards milling around.

As I approached, the old lady caught me out of the corner of her eye and greeted me with a warm but confused expression.

'I'm so sorry, I just walked off with it, without realising,' I shouted over the hum of announcements. I held the roll of notes in the air, putting her in the picture, and also the guard, whose pricked-up ears alerted me to his attention again. He watched from afar.

'Well, I'll be damned.' Her smile developed into a grin that revealed a perfect row of scintillating white dentures. She thanked me and took the money with an aged hand. She was wearing a charm bracelet like the one my mother used to wear, gold and old-fashioned, from another time.

I apologised again. Then I said, 'I hope the rest of your day runs a lot smoother.'

She laughed, and so did I. I couldn't help but wonder what her business was in London that day. She intrigued me. I would have loved to have asked more questions. I would have loved for it to be midday, and for her to have no plans, and me neither. I'd ask her to join me in a drink, she would accept, and we'd spend the rest of the afternoon discussing her life over a good bottle of something. Maybe more than one. Definitely more.

'Well, goodbye again,' I said. I made to walk off.

'You checked it's all there?' It was the guard, now upon us, no longer a haze in the foreground.

I turned around. 'What did you fucking say?'

'I told the lady to check her money.'

'You fucking what?'

'She doesn't know you, she just told me. I don't know you and I don't like you. Who knows who you are?'

'I'm the fucking guy that tried to help this lady out this morning. I'm the only fucking guy that stopped to see if she was OK. I could have ignored her this morning, like every other ignorant cunt chose to do.'

'Could have been a ploy. You might be an opportunist.'

The old lady, whose name I still didn't know and would probably never find out, waved the money in the air. 'It's all here,' she said. 'Seventy pounds, all present and correct.'

More than I'd thought.

I stared at the guard. He'd better be quick, because I wasn't going to give him much time. 'You owe me an apology.'

We stared at each other, a few seconds that felt like minutes.

She stood there motionless, watching, not sure whether to intervene.

The concourse had become quiet, that rare few

seconds in between trains. The old lady seemed lost, alone. It wouldn't be for long. Beyond her slender frame I could see the glow of headlamps as the next train eased into the station, followed by another on an adjacent platform. This would be my opportunity.

I gave the guard an opening. One last chance to put things right. One last chance to end this right now.

'You owe me an apology,' I repeated.

'I owe you nothing,' he said. 'Now run along, I have work to do'

He turned his back on me and made his way back to the platform, where the passengers were now marching towards us in droves. His bread and butter, my unsolicited audience.

I followed him, walking on past the old lady.

The rat race suddenly hit us hard; it was like swimming against a strong tide. I looked behind, watching their ignorance as they submerged the old lady completely. One second she was there, the next drowning in a sea of commuters.

I turned back towards the guard, keeping the lump of lard in my eyeline. I wanted to hurt him. I wanted to hurt him real bad.

3

Commuters swarmed around us, a mass of bodies.

Now was the chance to forget the madness and walk away, get the fuck out of there and continue today like I had the gazillion monotonous Mondays before. Nine-to-five – eat, sleep and repeat. But I didn't.

I had to act fast. I needed it to be right, and time was running out if I wanted to disappear into the crowd. I ran it all through my head. We were probably no more than eight feet apart. I edged closer, constantly brushing shoulders with an impatient public who didn't give a toss about my existence, drawn to their office blocks like sharks to blood.

My slow but evident approach alerted him to my presence. He turned and fixed his grey, soulless eyes on mine, then adopted a more rigid stance, as though expecting something to happen. He was right to assume so.

Five feet apart, we stood in everyone's way, squaring

up to each other like two cowboys from an old Western flick, waiting to draw. He seemed game and edged closer. Fool.

He was clenching his right fist so tight, you could see the veins pushing up through his skin. He had incredibly big hands. His fingers were covered in cheap gold sovereigns, his nails bitten so deep, the skin around them was broken and red raw.

I'm left-handed. One in ten people are. They say we're more intelligent, and that I believe. I'm in good company; Albert Einstein, Leonardo da Vinci and Winston Churchill were all left-handed. But then again, so were Jack the Ripper, the Boston Strangler and Osama bin Laden.

I'm predominantly left-handed, and not ambidextrous, like some. I do everything with it – write, smoke, eat, punch and masturbate. The whole fucking shebang. Jesus, come to think of it, if I ever lost my left arm I would be a bag of bones, craving nicotine, with balls like watermelons.

We were near enough toe-to-toe now. He wore heavy black boots, polished to Marine standards. I sensed he was ready to make the first move. I could almost hear the knuckles crack in his right hand. I could surprise him, being a southpaw, with a left hook, real sneaky, out of nowhere.

I used to box years ago, even managing a couple of white-collar fights. I won my first bout quite easy against a wiry Northerner who couldn't punch for toffee, but I got overconfident after that and came crashing back down to earth when I came up against a real hardened journeyman out of East London, an animal of a man who beat the living fucking daylights out of me.

Not long after that I gave it all up, the training replaced with binge-drinking sessions, the buzz of the ring replaced with a mix of narcotics.

The guard was really close now, all bad breath and stained teeth, flared nostrils and too much nasal hair. My personal space was invaded, my shadow merged with his. I took a step back to give me a few more seconds, weighed up my options and quickly put the left hook idea to bed. This geezer looked like he had anything but a glass jaw.

By stepping back I had given him an advantage, as I was now the perfect reach for a full-on blow to the head. He hesitated, maybe thinking about the consequences to his job. I couldn't get much from his stare. His intensions were hiding behind a gormless expression.

The confrontation had only been going on for a minute, but it felt like a week. Something, someone, had to give.

Then it did, and he made his first move, opening up

his body and slinging his right arm back, sort of slow motion. He was exposing himself to a body shot, but I held off. Far too much body mass for me to make a real impact. The guy must have weighed eighteen stone, an absolute giant of a man. His clenched fist was like a pendulum. It had now reached its extreme apex and was beginning to swing back towards me, with everything he had. This was the opportunity to end it.

I took a deep breath. One last chance to step away and get out of there. I didn't take it, though. The thought of what I was going to do, the pain it would inflict – I have to admit it exhilarated me. No, I wasn't going anywhere. This was happening. This would end.

His fist came bearing down on me, dumpy knuckles suggesting terrifying lumps of hard bone beneath, ready to crack my skull. Lucky for me he was no Muhammad Ali. His movement was sluggish and predictable. His fist came in at an angle, a blur of gold sovereigns out of the corner of my eye. I had to get it just right. Those years in the ring were not completely wasted. A millionth of a second before impact, I ducked out of the way.

Float like a butterfly, sting like a bee. The guard spiralled out of control. Total disorientation. It was as if he'd been hit himself and was searching for the ropes, legs like a new-born calf. He steadied himself, eventually, fifteen to twenty feet away, other side of the ring, dazed and dreamlike, unaware of his surroundings. I never took my eyes off him, waiting for his next move. Would there be one? Or was this it? I could have turned away and disappeared there and then. I didn't.

People stopped and stared, the final stragglers from the last two trains, the ones not as enthusiastic as the rest to get to their final destination. *My unsolicited audience.*

No one intervened. Yet.

We stood facing each other, a couple of gunslingers waiting to draw, our eyes fixed firmly on each other, no one in the world apart from us. A duel.

I was getting nothing from him. He just stood his ground, keeping his distance, a motionless pawn.

Come on, make your fucking move, arsehole.

I decided to egg him on, try and get a reaction, force him into something. I wasn't going to make the first move, the concourse would be laced with CCTV. Claim self-defence, let the jury decide.

'What you fucking waiting for? Come on, then. Scared you'll miss again, you fat bastard?'

That was all that was needed. It was like I sent him over the edge, any thoughts he had of walking away quashed. He came for me, like a raging bull.

For a fat bastard he moved pretty nimbly. In the blink of an eye he was upon me, breathing down on me, his face all screwed up, his eyes popping out of their sockets like a cartoon character. He made to punch me again, another sluggish swing with his right hand, slow and predictable like the first. If only his arms moved like his legs.

I could have ducked again, weaved out the way and moved on – but I didn't. As his lumpish hand came bearing down on my temple for a second time, I reached into my top pocket, pulled out the Stanley knife, switched the blade into place and ran it down the side of his face.

He instantly bellowed in agony, crashing down to his knees, the hand against the wound smothered in a dark, globby blood.

'What the hell have you done?' an elderly woman screamed.

'Jesus Christ!' howled a young guy with a thick black beard and oval-rimmed glasses. He was carrying a large backpack, both straps over his arms, the contents of his life. I wished I was going where he was right now. What the fuck had I done? Did I care? I wasn't sure. Was I?

More and more people gathered, my unsolicited audience growing by the second.

Two middle-aged women, receptionists chained to a 9-to-5 in smart corporate-coloured blazers and knee-high skirts, broke from the crowd to attend to the guard. Three younger men, all mid-thirties I would say, dressed in suits with stylish overcoats, made a beeline for me, their steady footsteps in a line, the taller of the three in the middle – the ringleader, the one who would make the first move. They were now within six feet of me, edging closer and closer. Everyone else formed a circle around us, taking me back to my school days when fights would break out in the playground: a circle of kids, pumped up on sugar, inciting a reluctant challenger against the year's toughest boy.

I was right, it was the tall one who made the first move. He stepped out of line, away from the other two, while they dropped in neatly behind. I weighed up my options quickly. There was no way I could take on all three of these guys, and even if I did, I would then have the remaining Joe Public against me. I had no time for a fight – I needed to escape. I made up my mind. I was ready for him.

Two feet away now, with his accomplices nestled in his shadow. They moved together. They moved well. One foot away, he stopped the attack with a raised hand.

'Don't move an inch, fella, otherwise we'll come down on you like a ton of bricks. You're coming with us, and I suggest you make it easy. Three of us, one of you. Now put the knife down, you sick bastard. We'll take a lot more stopping than an old man. Look at him. Whatever your issues were, he never deserved that.'

I was holding the blade out in front of me again. I

hadn't realised – a knee-jerk reaction. I tossed it aside like I was a captured soldier across enemy lines.

We all took time to stare across at the guard. He was still rolling around, screaming in agony. The two middle-aged women, now assisted by several others, including other station staff, were all trying to calm him down. It wasn't working.

I felt no remorse. I was sure of that now. I didn't know if it was the comedown from the drugs or just me, but I was glad I did it. I was glad I shut him up.

The tall guy now made his move, stepping away from the other two and trying to grab me by the arm. I managed to shrug him off. He came again, this time with both arms raised, as though ready to throttle me. He never even got close. I lashed out with my right leg. The abrupt movement wasn't spontaneous but controlled. It had to be controlled to deliver the impact I required. My loafer smashed up into his groin. The impact felt good. I'd connected better than I expected. He fell to his knees, like the guard before him. This was getting easy. I didn't give him a second chance.

As he groaned in pain I grabbed his hair, a pathetic ponytail, and pulled his head towards my knee, powering into his chin as hard as possible. I let go and he collapsed beneath me in a pool of blood. I must have broken his jaw.

The backup seemed startled. They both took a slight

step back, their hands raised like they were honouring the Queensberry rules. I wasn't going to stick around to find out their division. I scouted the crowd. The circle had moved in closer. I could almost feel their heated breaths upon my skin. I observed for a weakness, and saw it.

Three young schoolgirls around thirteen years old stood in line, forming part of the circle. Two shared headphones, taking an earpiece each, the other was chomping hard on chewing gum, revealing bad teeth and silver braces. They were watching intently, like it was some sort of role play at a shitty school fête. They all wore the same uniform, dull brown blazers with pleated skirts, mustard yellow shirts and short, messy ties.

I left the tall guy groaning beneath me. His confederates backed off for now, regrouping, plotting their next move. I gave them no option. I headed straight towards the young trio. It would be harsh, but I had no time to be sympathetic. It would hurt at least two of them, but it wouldn't be critical, and I had no other choice. The circle of people were moving in as the two young men regained their confidence and began walking towards me again, with angry faces but wary eyes.

I ran at pace. Using my shoulder as a barrier, I knocked the two young girls sharing the headset to the ground. They landed heavily. One cracked her head against the concrete floor.

I was sure she'd be OK, wouldn't she? Would she?

I was free for now, which was my only concern. I didn't stop running, I didn't look back. I accelerated onto the station concourse, creating a stir. People's heads turned from the departure board, from coffee stalls, escalators, ticket machines – everywhere, a concourse of eyewitnesses. Their faces were indistinguishable. A dream.

I zigzagged through them, knowing they would be giving chase.

The fox and the hounds.

I found a short staircase and jumped down it. I found a row of barriers and jumped over them. I headed through a maze of tunnels, running as fast as I could. My lungs began to burn, and my legs began to ache.

I kept going, my mind a fog, no real sense of where I was heading, just a rabbit warren of never-ending tunnels. I never turned back, not even once.

The tunnels seemed to get smaller, the white tiled walls closing in around me. I kept going, out of breath, my body weak; I felt like I was going to pass out any second.

They were close, but how close?

Would I make it? Would I? Wouldn't I? And even if I did, how long before they picked me up on CCTV? If I did get away I could never go back home. It would only be a matter of time before they came for me – a dawn raid, a dozen men, a warrant for my arrest.

The thought was terrifying. The sheer realisation of what I had done and the consequences that I would have to endure – my life over in a flash, and not on my own terms.

I would have given up, faced the truth of my spiralling downfall, a bitter end to a pointless life; I would have admitted defeat, stopped running – turned and faced my pursuers with my hands held high and the look of a condemned man. I would have done just that. I would have, but I didn't. I didn't because I had the smidgen of an idea, a remote possibility – the last chance saloon.

I kept going.

The floor beneath me now felt like quicksand. I'd slowed considerably and was panting like a fucking dog locked in a car on a blistering, sunny day. I turned left, I turned right, every footstep now met with exquisite pain as my body began to resist my advance.

What if one of the guards had radioed ahead? Maybe they were coming at me in all directions, homing in on me from every fucking angle.

I needed to get out of the station quickly if I were to have any chance. It had already been far too long. I reached some escalators descending deeper into the

Underground and joined them. My pathway to hell?

The escalators led into a small space about ten metres square. Directly opposite them was a wall with two maps indicating the destinations of the two platforms, left and right, each platform reachable through two arches chiselled into the brickwork running parallel to the back wall.

I stood for a second. The air was dense, the pungent smell of the Underground all around me. I looked left. I looked right. Two platforms crammed with bodies, not a fag paper between them. I turned around for the first time, looking up towards the top of the escalator. There they were – the hounds. There were four of them – the two remaining smart guys closely followed by two station guards.

I looked left again. I looked right again. Two platforms infested with the human race, an irritating swarm of individuals unaware of the quandary I found myself in.

They were halfway down the escalator, a quartet gunning for my blood – I chose the left platform.

My decision was made by a slim, thirty-something brunette. She wore a summer dress just above the knee, and a pair of patent heels that reflected the artificial light in the underworld we were all currently living our minutes in. She had great legs, tanned. A heavy coat was draped over her left arm; her nails had a French manicure; her wedding finger glittered with two carats. Engaged! Lucky man. She was standing sideways, directly under the arch, looking down the platform, while listening to music through discreet wireless headphones. She was tapping her foot.

***

Another time, in a different world, I would have ridden the Underground to the end of the line in the wrong direction to try my luck with this woman. I'd been a vainglorious man once, before the drugs and alcohol took their toll. I'd stopped looking after myself. Didn't give a shit. Occasionally I would catch myself in a mirror and still see those soulful eyes in my haggard reflection.

I'd always been confident around women and nine times out of ten had my pick of the bunch, and often did – rock or no rock. I was a bastard. I followed my cock about like a dog on heat, a real cavalier who never gave a fuck about the repercussions. Penny.

My dear Penny; I did love her but I could never help myself. One day I would stop and be the loyal husband she deserved. Give up the coke and get a life. I would do it, for sure. Wouldn't I?

Today was different. Hell, was it. It was not another time, it was not a different world. The present was a cunt, a living fucking nightmare I was seeking desperately to get out of. The brunette was my answer, but for no other reason than her hair. Her hair was straight, past shoulder length, well-looked-after. It shone, was in great condition, and plenty of body. I bet it smelled great. A two hundred-pound cut from a lavish salon, nice guys with plenty of chat, great physiques, snug black T-shirts. Chewing gum, glistening smiles, long hair on top shaped into lavish styles, tight back and sides shaved to the blade with the ultimate accuracy...

My mind, it wandered. It often did, constantly in another place.

I glanced back. They were close. Too fucking close. Three-quarters of the way down the escalator.

I staggered towards the platform, my legs heavy, like I'd just completed an Ironman race. I was running on empty.

Left platform over right.

It was now or never.

4

I continued down the platform, jostling through a disgruntled public.

'Watch where you're going.'

'We all want to get somewhere, mate.'

'Oi, you ignorant pig.'

Fuck 'em.

The wind built up within the tunnel, the warm air pushing hard against my neck. I continued until I could continue no further, and slumped within the crowd at the far end of the platform. I peered back.

The dark inner depths of the adjacent tunnel began to show signs of light, and the rails in front of me began to sing from the vibration of the approaching carriages. I thought of my thirty-something-year-old and how she'd made up my mind – left platform over right. I'd left her behind but her face would remain in my memory, for how long I don't know. Long enough, I hoped, to be able to fantasise – and I would for sure, given the chance.

The Tube accelerated out of the tunnel like a bullet from a barrel, booming and aggressive. The whites of the driver's eyes, exaggerated in his dimly lit cabin, were fixed firmly ahead.

The gentle breeze that had flicked the thirty-something's hair only a few seconds ago now gushed around the platform. The air felt good against my perspiring skin. My mouth was dry, my head felt light. I drifted for a second, but only a second. A commotion had erupted towards the centre of the platform, alerting me to their consistent presence.

Four men would carve their way through a crowd a lot easier than one, like a fat kid through a ball pit of M&M's.

Most of the carriages were now in the station. I could see the driver's face quite clearly as his cabin eased towards me – three, two, one metre away. He was a youngish guy with a number five buzz cut. He wore a gold hoop earring and had at least a week's stubble. He looked bored, to the point of distraction. Too many trips down far too many tunnels.

The brakes hissed as the steel wheels locked against the track beneath them, the sound echoing around the platform. The people around me shuffled their feet as they altered their stances, the ones at the front broadening their shoulders to emphasise their position in the pecking order. Just like earlier this morning. The 07:26, before the shit hit the fan. It seemed a fucking lifetime ago.

The doors to the Tube opened, people spilled out of the congested carriages, dog-eat-dog.

I gazed along the platform. The quartet were struggling against the commuters who were pushing and shoving in the opposite direction, each one transfixed, destined for the same day they'd lived a thousand times.

The carriage had emptied out considerably. I was dripping in sweat from fear and exhaustion. If they made it to the carriage it would be over. I would have no chance against four, and there would be nowhere to run once the doors closed. Trapped – over.

For what might be my final thoughts as a free man I never thought about Penny, or the once good times in my life – a normal life with friends and family, a life I would never have again. Instead, I thought about prison, with its claustrophobic cells, and the men with no hope. I thought about my sentence, which would be longer than I could ever handle. I would never last. I thought about suicide and how I could attempt it with minimum resources. A razor blade to my wrists, a crude and catastrophic end to my short life. I flashed back to when I was a kid – a good father and mother, a great childhood with wonderful memories. How did I get here? It felt as if I was dreaming. I was sure to wake up soon to the warmth of Penny's breath on my skin, her arms locked around my body in a perfect world.

The beeping of the closing doors brought me back, to the first carriage of twelve, a hot and sticky Underground, the present. I breathed a deep sigh of relief as I saw the doors begin to close in front of me. The feeling was short-lived, as he came from nowhere – the taller of the two smart gents, the one with the more athletic build, the one who'd led the chase. The one who would just not fucking give up, the T-1000 from *Terminator 2*. He had broken from the pack, leaving the others trailing in his desperate bid to reach me. A good citizen, for King and country, a true hero.

An annoying cunt.

He leaped from the platform towards the closing doors, his eyes never leaving mine, with a look of intrepidity.

I took a step back and waited, my fists raised, ready for one last fight. This bastard was going to get my last drop of vitality. I took a deep breath and waited some more, but what happened next was unanticipated – the doors shut across him.

'Fuck,' he screamed, through a wash of saliva. I felt the anger and animosity within him.

It was the first time I'd seen him up close. He was fair, a scattering of freckles across the bridge of his nose.

He had a dusting of stubble and pale blue eyes; his hair was natural without product. As he growled some more he revealed a perfect row of veneers.

He seemed fit and strong. My initial estimation of his age showed him some injustice – he was more late twenties than mid-thirties. He was smart, ready for another day in the office – a white shirt and slim, navy blue woven tie, with a neat half-Windsor knot resting tight against a cutaway collar.

I stared for what could only have been a couple of seconds but which felt more like minutes, watching him struggle as he flailed desperately against the automatic sliding doors that had wedged him in. They had compressed against his torso, and he had one leg and one arm within the carriage. He thrashed like a trapped python in his bid for freedom.

Why hadn't the driver realised? Opened the doors?

I was directly opposite him, no more than five feet away, the only person standing on the carriage. Everyone else remained seated, panic-stricken, afraid to intervene.

The pretty boy's gritty resistance eventually paid off, and the driver was alerted that one of his doors hadn't closed, maybe by a flashing red light within the dashboard of his cab. Whatever the reason, and to my trepidation, the doors opened.

A sinister smile broke across his face as he stepped

into the carriage, like the cat got the cream.

'Nowhere further to run.' His voice was gravelly and unexpected.

I weighed up my options. There weren't many – kill or be killed.

He stood within the doorframe, six foot plus, well-built – from a generation of gym fanatics. His eyes never left mine. Total focus – ready to take me down.

'Come on, then, what you fucking waiting for?' There was an unflinching tone to my voice. I had nothing to lose. One last dance.

'You have two choices, my friend. You either come quietly or have me to deal with.'

Who was this fucking guy? Seriously.

One, two, three, right on cue, the surplus dregs of the quartet rolled in behind him like the members of a disfigured boy band. He turned and faced them then he turned back and faced me.

'Actually, make that come quickly or deal with us,' he said smugly. Like the cat got the cream, the mouse and the holiday home in Barbados.

One of the guards was on his radio. He then spoke to the guy already on the train.

'We've stopped the Tube, he isn't going anywhere. Transport Police are on their way.'

'So what's it going to be? The easy way or the hard

way?' My impatient nemesis calling the shots. He edged closer.

I'd made a mistake, a big fucking mistake, and my plan was disintegrating with every passing second. Escaping by Tube would have worked if they hadn't seen me approach it – board it. I should have been quicker – got out of sight, then got on a Tube. There were so many platforms and different lines down here, they would never have been able to trace me. I was sure of it. The difference was they did see me, and within their jurisdiction they had the power to control things – CCTV, trains, Tubes. They had me under their spell at the flick of a radio switch. I wasn't smart enough, I wasn't thinking straight. As soon as they saw me I should have tried to make it out of the station, get above ground, out of their world – then I would have had a chance, a chance for my idea to maybe work. Would it have? Wouldn't it have?

Everything was a blur, and I was knee-deep in shit. I'd made the wrong decisions. Christ, I'd made the wrong decisions. But I had no choice, there was no way back now. I had to keep going, I had to keep trying.

'Well?' The smart guy, the leader of the pack.

'I think I'll try the hard way,' I said.

'What the fuck?'

I smashed my elbow up through his nostrils and followed through to the bridge of his nose – everything I had left, my full weight behind it. It took him by surprise. He stumbled back into the arms of his clan.

I ran along the carriage, as fast as I possibly could, a new-found energy feeding on the slim hope my idea was still alive. He gave chase, of course he did. I knew I wouldn't stop him – six foot tall and built like a brick shit-house. I'd gained a few valuable seconds though. A few valuable seconds to get ahead.

I was probably half a carriage in front. They pursued in a neat line of four, the big guy in front, blood pissing from his nose, his face screwed up in rage. There'd been an announcement the train was out of service. People were getting off, worrying about how to get to work, not worrying about us, therefore no one to intervene. No last-gasp hero. London. No one gave a shit.

I kept going. My chest felt tight, my lungs about to explode and my legs like they had anchors tied around them. I passed through two carriages. They were gaining ground as the connecting doors between the cars slowed me down. These doors weren't meant to be used, except in an emergency, so you had the very manual process of sliding down the window to then twist the door open from the outside, before stepping across the car and opening the door into the next carriage. I was also closing both doors each time so they had to repeat the process. I was staying ahead – just – but where was I fucking going?

I was running out of carriages fast, and the adjacent platform was blocked by a mass of infuriated bodies gunning to reach their next destination. Like me... but how? At this rate I was heading straight to jail: Do Not Pass Go, Do Not Collect £200.

Fuck it, die trying. I approached the next carriage and peered over my shoulder with a flick of the neck. Quarter of a carriage now. Harder to shake off than an STD.

I opened the door and shut it behind me, but this time I didn't open the door to the next carriage. Instead, I turned back towards the door I'd just closed and, using the open window frame as a ledge for my foot, pulled myself up onto the roof of the train and ran in the opposite direction, over their heads.

It was fucking ludicrous, but it worked. By the time brick-shit-house guy stumbled up to join me I was over a carriage away. I could hear the radio conversation now.

'Our suspect is on the roof of the train. All available guards immediately to Central Line platform 2. I repeat, our suspect is on the roof of the train.'

Somewhere else, two guards were chewing the fat over a coffee break.

'Did he just say the roof of the fucking train?'

'He sure did, my friend.'

The people on the platform glanced up, their original frustration now diluted by the events unfolding in front of their very eyes.

I was back where I started, adjacent to the archway leading to the small, ten-metre space containing the escalators – above the platform, looking down on the faces staring up at me in disbelief. I turned to my right. Brick shit-house eased his way towards me, his arms away from his body to steady himself. He was half a carriage away now and close enough for me to see the determination in his face. I glanced back down. I looked back at him. I glanced back down. I jumped.

I scraped myself up off the floor like a burnt fried egg out of a frying pan. I could hardly stand. A middle-aged guy – smart camel coat and a large aluminium briefcase – lay sprawled out beneath me, holding his shoulder and wincing. He'd taken the brunt of my fall. Unfortunate, but not my problem. I glanced up. I took a look around. The exit was directly in front of me, through a rabble of compressed bodies – a defiant wall of flesh between me and an interim freedom.

I felt hot. Boiling. I felt claustrophobic. I felt debilitated. I didn't feel like me. It didn't feel like Monday morning. I glimpsed back up towards the roof of the carriage. There he was in all his glory, hanging over me like a dark rain cloud.

'Stop him!' he screamed at the very top of his voice.

I turned back round. A willowy twenty-something

guy in jeans and a hoodie was coming towards me. His long blonde hair was matted into dreads. He appeared like he hadn't washed for a month.

'Stop right there, brother,' he said, in a drawn-out, lazy way. He was covered in dry paint. An apprentice of some sort – cash in hand for weed and computer games.

'Fucking grab him.' That voice again, ingrained in my head. The guy who wouldn't just give it up. I was determined it would be the last time I ever heard it.

I leaned down and picked up the aluminium briefcase. It was heavy, probably full of important documents waiting to be signed. Not today. I swung it hard into the side of the dreadlock kid's face. He fell like a domino.

I didn't waste a second. Not for the first time today, and I was guessing not the last, time was of the essence. I grabbed the case with both hands and held it in front of my face. I then charged at the crowd before me like an exhausted soldier attacking no man's land. No hope, no fear.

'You've fucking let him through!' That voice. Again. Was I hearing right? Surely not. Impossible. Wasn't it?

I'd closed my eyes and hoped for the best, but as I opened them I found I was now standing in the ten-metre square space below the escalators. I glanced back at the archway leading to the platform. There was a gap in the crowd, a clear path leading directly to the train.

47

Either side of the path people were scattered across the floor, a confusion of bodies dazed in the aftermath of my destruction.

Beyond and above them was the unusual figure of a man standing on the roof of a train. Our eyes met. For the first time I saw defeat in his expression. I smiled back at him – nothing sinister, just the faint assertion that I was his victor. I placed the case on the floor and ran up the escalator, my legs heavy and weak, and managed to find my way back to the concourse. I couldn't see the guard. I imagined him in the back of an ambulance, still screaming in pain. He would be scarred for life.

I had to get out of the station, the concourse, the goddam city. They would be zooming in on me now, fucking CCTV everywhere, some slothful operator in his ideal job, sitting on his arse, watching my every move.

I found an exit taking me back to street level. Outdoors, I was met by a downpour that had everyone running for cover. The sky was grey and dense, the rain thick, each individual droplet exploding on the pavement.

The slothful operator would be telling the transport police I was now outside the station. I took a look around. Cameras everywhere, the world watching, my very own Truman show. I hailed a black cab and got the fuck out of there.

The rain hit the roof of the cab hard, breaking the

silence between me and the driver. I was in no mood for small talk. Outside, the world was a blur, just the glow of car headlamps and traffic lights breaking through the condensation covering the windows.

I couldn't believe my idea was still on the table – a possibility, an outside chance, for sure. But this was far from over. For all I knew they could be watching the cab now, watching every street I turned into. I kept looking behind expecting blue flashing lights, but every time I did there was nothing.

I thought about what I was going to do next – the idea and the things I needed to do first to make it happen, or at least give it a chance of happening. Was I deluded? Was I insane to think I could actually get away with this? Before I could think any further we ground to a halt.

'That will be £15.50, guv.'

What? We were there? I couldn't believe I'd made it this far. I gave the driver a twenty and told him to keep the change, then stood on the kerb watching the taxi disappear, another vehicle in the congestion. The rain was still heavy; I was soaked through but didn't move. Instead, I checked out my surroundings. No SWAT team telling me to get on the ground and put my hands behind my back. No sound of propeller blades humming above me as a chopper homed in on my location. Nothing. Nothing at all. I stepped away from the kerb and glanced up at my destination. Above me in bold red lettering was the word 'Dreamfield'. I strolled into the complex through glass sliding doors, fantasizing of what might still be.

Dreamfield is a large shopping centre on the outskirts of the city. Inside was new and fresh, only a few years old. In front of me was a parade of glitzy shops as far as the eye could see, people darting in and out of them weighed down with bags and low bank balances.

I peered up; I glanced around. More CCTV. If they hadn't traced me to the shopping centre I would be OK, as the CCTV in here would be run by some private security team. Yes, the police could gain footage after an event, but right now, at this moment in time, I was out of their jurisdiction. I still had to be quick, though. No time for complacency. If they had managed to catch me going into the shopping centre, some other slothful operator would be hunting me down right now, and it wouldn't be long before the police were here.

I needed to change my appearance, and I needed to find somewhere that would supply the stuff I required. I started walking.

I eventually came across a store that would do – a big department store, one that did a bit of everything. I headed to menswear, where I bought a pair of jeans and a sweatshirt, and a pair of trainers, black, the running type.

After that I headed to a different floor and purchased an electric razor, and some batteries to go with it.

I came across a toilet, found an empty cubicle and closed the door, then changed out of my wet clothes and into the new ones. Sitting on the toilet I began to hack at my hair and beard with the razor. After ten minutes I had a number three buzz cut and a five o'clock shadow. I left the cubicle, dumped my clothes and the razor in a bin and checked myself over in the mirror. My reflection reminded me of the days of my treatment, after the chemo had really kicked in, waking each morning to a pillow full of hair. When we first shaved my head, Penny and I, it was the first time I'd thought about dying. Without Penny I would never have got through it. Beating cancer should have been the turning point in my life, God's way of telling me he'd given me another chance. I should have grasped it with both hands and appreciated everything I had.

I stared hard at myself, looking beyond my despondent reflection. What had I become? How did it get to this? I wished I had the answers, I really did, but now wasn't the time for self-pity, and now wasn't the time to reflect on the collapse of my life.

Right now I was knee-deep in shit. Right now I had to deal with getting myself out of the fucking mess I, and no one else, had created. I turned and left my past within the mirror; I had today to deal with.

Outside it was still raining. I hailed a cab, gave the driver my destination and settled into my seat, on edge. A bag of nerves. Every so often I'd check behind for blue flashing lights, but nothing.

The twenty-minute drive felt like an eternity. By the time we reached my destination, my body was covered in a cold sweat that began seeping through the cotton of my top, revealing dark damp patches against the light grey, like I'd just finished a 10k run.

'You alright, mate?' the driver asked, as we exchanged money. 'You don't look too well.'

'Think I'm coming down with something. I'll be fine.'

He made to give me my change.

'Keep it,' I said.

'Why, thank you very much. Get yourself home and tucked up in bed, if you know what's best for you.'

'I will, thanks.'

If only he knew.

The rain had eased to nothing but a fine drizzle. I was in front of an expansive train station. St Pancras.

My passport had given me the idea. They wouldn't expect me to have it with me. The police, that is. I mean, who carried a passport around with them just travelling to work? I would have been described to them as an average commuter, just a guy heading to the office. I might have been going on a business trip, an overnight stay, or even a few days tying up deals in some cosmopolitan city drenched in European sunshine, but I had no suitcase, overnight bag, or even the suggestion of a rucksack. No, they wouldn't expect me to be leaving the country. I had that in my locker. One up. A slight advantage. Well, for now, at the very least.

I was supposed to meet the loan shark after work, some pub east of here, a rough neighbourhood just out of town. They would be waiting for me – a bundle of dirty cash loaned at a staggering rate, and my life if it wasn't paid back on time. They would be pissed I hadn't shown. I didn't care. I wasn't going to be around to reap the repercussions.

I found a bank and drained our joint account. Just over seven grand, everything I had in the world. I'd only got paid today, same as Penny. It was the only time each month our account had anything in it before the debt bled it dry. Every bill would now bounce, including the mortgage. I was leaving Penny in a mess. I had no choice.

The ticket hall was surprisingly empty. I was next in line after an old couple with too much luggage and after about two minutes was waved down to my place by a young blonde who'd just opened a new counter. She asked me to bear with her, so I did. The old couple was at the next counter; he did the talking while she took a back seat. She smiled at me and I smiled back.

I waited nervously. They would be out there still, CCTV everywhere, looking for my whereabouts. But they would be looking for a man in office attire, with long hair and a beard, not a guy in a sweatshirt, jeans and trainers. Not a guy with a number three buzz cut. The thought eased my mind ever so slightly.

I got my phone out of my pocket and texted Penny. I said sorry. That was it. I waited for the message to send, and as soon as it did I switched the phone off. I would dump it before leaving.

'Sorry about that, sir,' she said. She had beautiful green eyes that lit up an average face. 'How can I help?'

'One way ticket to the Gare de Lyon, please.'

'Sure, sir, and when would you like that for?'

'The next available one, please.'

The train was due to leave at 11:05 am. I boarded half hour before departure and located my seat but I didn't sit down. Instead, I made my way towards the buffet car and bought a bottle of wine. Red. Nothing else.

On making my way back to my seat I found the old couple I'd seen in the ticket hall were sitting opposite me. We laughed at the coincidence before settling into the journey. She read a Jane Austen novel while he shuffled around the *Telegraph*.

The train left on time. My wine was OK, just OK. Before we'd even hit the tunnel, it was gone. I slept for the rest of the journey, filtering in and out of dreams that I didn't remember.

5

I awoke somewhere I assumed to be on the outskirts of Paris. Lush green fields flicked past the window on what was a dreary day here, too, but in another country.

The old couple were asleep, mouths open, catching flies. An announcement was made, first in French and then in English, informing passengers we would soon be approaching the Gare de Lyon, which produced a wave of activity as people flustered for their luggage.

I stayed in my seat, with no luggage to contend with. A jerk against the rails disturbed and then woke the old couple. She marked her page in her book with a leather bookmark and gave it to her husband, who put it away in a large carpet-bag that had seen better days.

The natural light cutting through the carriage was suddenly cut off as we hit a short tunnel, fluorescent tubes replacing a weak sun. I stood up and bid the old couple a safe onward journey, which they both reciprocated. If only they knew.

I waited eagerly by the doors and thought about what I was going to do next. A hotel, a good one. Definitely five-star. What the fuck. I had seven grand; it wouldn't go far, but I wanted a few days to think about what I was going to do next. They would eventually find out I took a Eurostar to Paris but by then it would be too late. Once the money ran out, I didn't have a clue. For now I was just grateful for my freedom and I was going to enjoy the next few days, at least. After that I didn't care. Did I?

I thought about smoking. I was desperate for a drag – my whole body craved nicotine.

The doors to the train opened and I was greeted by a group of kids with smiles that curled to the bottom of their ears. Next stop Marne-la-Vallée – Chessy, Disneyland, Mickey Mouse and all things nice.

They didn't wait for me to get off, just scuttled around me with a vibrant energy, high on life, nothing to fear. An innocence I envied. Proud parents made way for my exit, apologising for their children.

'Not a problem,' I said, and stepped off the train, looking for the nearest exit, ever so desperate for a drag.

I was standing on the steps of the Gare de Lyon smoking my second cigarette twenty minutes later. I'd stopped and exchanged all the money I had on me, which was about £6,800-odd after the train ticket. The exchange got me 7,300 Euro and a dusting of coins.

It wasn't going to last long, but I would make sure I enjoyed every last cent.

I soaked up Paris there and then, breathing it in with deep glugs of air. I watched, I listened. I stubbed my cigarette butt against a stone step and started to walk into the world I was just observing thinking back to London. It seemed so long ago – weeks, months, years – but only a few hours.

I probably walked for about five minutes in no real direction, just turning into streets as I came across them. I'd drifted past several hotels but the Royal made me stop and take note. It was beautiful, elegant, a five-star hotel with real presence. The front was simple but stylish, having four floors, each one the same in a perfect harmonious proportion and balance. Four rooms one each level, four French doors leading onto a wrought-iron balcony, each one shaded by a striped canopy of white and lavender.

The Royal would do nicely. I would stay three or four nights and live a little on what I had. I was sure they would have caught up with me by then.

There was no one on reception, so I rang the bell. It didn't take long for a pretty thing to appear and greet me in her native tongue. She was young, twenty-one at a push, probably in her first job. She wore hardly any make-up, but didn't need to.

'Good afternoon, do you have a room for four nights?'

'Have you made a reservation, monsieur?'

'No, I haven't.'

She began to type away at the computer on the desk – one of three, the other two vacant. Maybe lunch time?

After about a minute she peered up from the screen. She had great eyes, a deep brown. Mysterious.

'We have two types of rooms available for the next four nights, a single room or a deluxe suite.'

'Single room will be fine.'

She disappeared into her screen again and typed away at her keyboard, punching keys at an impressive speed.

'Can I take your name please, monsieur?' she said, without raising her head.

'Sure.' I gave her my name. I'd thought about using a false one but then realised she'd want to see my passport for ID as I'd be paying with cash. I knew it was risky, handing over my identity. The Old Bill back home must have realised by now I'd taken the Eurostar and traced me purchasing a ticket or have a record of me at passport control. However, Europe was a big place, and how did they know I'd stayed in Paris? I had no other choice as I wasn't spending my last days as a free man cooped up in some rundown hostel.

'That comes to a total of 1,299 Euro. How will you be paying today?'

'Cash.'

'Cash is fine, monsieur, but I'll need a card as a deposit, just against incidentals.'

I'd known it was coming. If they swiped my card, it would get declined. I'd had prepared for the question.

'My wife has travelled on to Marne-la-Vallée, Disneyland, with the kids.' I put my hand out and held it just below my waistline to show the height of my imaginary children. 'My wife has mistakenly taken my credit cards with her. Although I don't think it was a mistake, eh?'

She laughed.

'I can give you 1,000 Euro to hold, plus the rate for the four nights on top.' I stared at the girl's name tag, placed with precision across the pocket of a navy blue blazer with gold buttons. She wore a loose silk scarf and had an extra button undone on her crisp white shirt, to reveal a small silver cross. 'Azurine. That's a beautiful name.'

She gave an ironic lift of the brow. She'd seen and heard it all before. She had amazing cheekbones, great skin.

'I will just need to check with my manager.'

I didn't like that she thought I was hitting on her when I mentioned her name. She was old enough to be my daughter and I didn't want to be that sleazy guy. So I lied. I was getting pretty good at it.

'Your name – you didn't let me finish. I find it beautiful because it's also my daughter's name.'

'Your daughter is called Azurine? Why did you give your daughter a French name?'

'Because it's beautiful.'

She laughed. 'How old is she?'

'She'll be nine in May. She would like you. She would think you're a princess. Thanks for your help, Azurine.'

Azurine smiled, a warm enchanting smile. I was no longer that sleazy guy. She went out into the office at the back, returning after about two minutes.

'Cash is fine. I'll just need to see a driving licence or passport for proof of identification.'

I slid my passport across the counter and waited with bated breath as she opened it. She seemed to stare at it for ages. My heart was in my mouth, my hands clammy, my brow covered in beads of sweat.

'That's all fine, monsieur. If you could just sign here, please.'

I let out a huge sigh of relief.

'Everything OK, monsieur?'

'Yes, fine. Sorry, been a long day.'

'Well, you can rest now. Here is your key. So with the deposit that will be 2,299 Euro, please.'

I handed over the money and got directions to my room, then made my way along a corridor and entered a lobby with six lifts. I pressed a button and one opened immediately.

I thought about how Azurine never questioned me for not having any luggage, not even an overnight bag. Maybe they were on to me? Maybe it was entrapment? I was overthinking it. There was no way that was possible so soon. Was it?

I reached my floor and counted down the doors until my number. The room was warm and elegant, decorated with fine antiques, and had a nice clean feel. It was spacious, with a wooden floor, walls painted in delicate neutral colours, and a great natural light. I stepped over to the window to a picturesque view out of the front of the hotel and down onto the rue de Berri. I took a second to observe an old Parisian man roll some tobacco as he took five on a bench surrounded by what seemed like heavy grocery bags. He licked his fag papers into place and sparked up with a match, then inhaled, sat back and blew a cloud of grey smoke out into the afternoon air. I could almost feel the hit of nicotine.

I stepped back across the room, took two clear money bags from the bureau de change out of my back pockets and placed them on the bedside cabinet. I undid one and counted out 2,000 Euro on the bed. They were crisp, fresh notes, twenties and fifties, a mixture of bright blues and oranges. I folded them, put them in my back pocket and stowed the remaining money in the safe.

On leaving the room I took the stairs this time, bidding Azurine a pleasant day as I passed her at the reception. She'd now been joined by two ladies in the same uniform, older, not as pretty. At the main entrance a young porter tipped his hat in my direction. He wore a green overcoat with matching fur trim and large gold buttons. I bid him a good day, stepped through the revolving door and made my way out onto the streets of Paris.

6

Outside, I immediately put a flame to a cigarette. It tasted good. I passed the old man on the bench, who was now capturing forty winks under a tilted panama hat, then turned a corner, then another, wandering a smart street for about half a mile or so, before heading right, into a cobbled alley. No real sense of direction. I was just waiting to stumble across my destination. The alley was filled with café bars and bistros. People spilled out onto the street, clustered around tables with stylish metal heaters, chain-smoking in between sips of good coffee.

I walked some more, passing a bistro with a bright orange canopy. A large, smartly dressed man sat alone at a small round table edged into the front window. He wore a sky blue polo shirt and pink chinos and was speaking into a cell phone wedged between his double chin and shoulder. It was an older type of phone, black, with a small display screen. I imagined it was a business call. He spoke with his hands, emphasising points and conveying enthusiasm, interrupted by glugs of what seemed like a good Chardonnay, judging by the rich yellow glow. He had a plate of food that wouldn't look out of place on an artist's easel – a large, succulent red lobster, so fresh it seemed about to crawl off the plate. I moved on. More bistros and more café bars. I explored further, twisting with the direction of the alley, undulating with a generous spring in my step through the heartbeat of the city.

Eventually I reached a T-junction. I gazed left, then right, and decided right, directed by the Eiffel Tower spiralling into the heavy clouds above, and now always in my eyeline. It took another two cigarettes and possibly half a mile before I found what I was looking for. I flicked my fag in the gutter and entered a shop, my introduction announced by a large bell hanging over an old wooden door.

The shop was empty. I could smell the oak from the neat fittings, dozens of shelves lined with multiple coloured garments in a combination of fine materials, folded to perfection. Rails hung with the finest suits, arranged by colour from light to dark. In the middle of the floor was an elevated display of classic shoes, brogues, derbies and loafers in leathers and suedes. Alongside sat a tan chesterfield where customers could sit and try on the unique designs. The lighting was a warm, golden glow projected from three heavy silver chandeliers that hung from a high ceiling and divided the room into a near perfect symmetry.

A man appeared from a door behind the counter at the back of the store – a small skinny man, well into his late sixties, with jet black hair that was slightly receding and slicked to one side. He was wearing a silver grey waistcoat with a gold pocket watch; his shirt was a deep pink with the sleeves rolled up. His trousers were black, his shoes patent leather with tassels. He had a tape measure draped around his neck, ready for business.

He approached, waltzing about on his toes, and stared me up and down. 'Bonjour, monsieur,' he said, in a soft voice.

I explained that my luggage had got lost and I needed some clothes to see me over the next few days.

This seemed to excite the man in front of me. He whirled around me like a ballet dancer with his tape measure. Before I knew it I had an armful of clothes to try on and was being whisked away to a private dressing room. We spoke over a drawn curtain, talking about me at first, nothing but a fabricated tale. Then we spoke about him, his life. He was interesting. His English was good. Better than my French.

'What is your name, sir? I like to call all my customers by their first name.'

I told him and asked him his own.

'My name is Charlemagne.'

'What a great name. If reincarnation is a thing I would love to come back as a Charlemagne.'

He laughed and thanked me.

I spent the next twenty minutes or so trying on an array of different clothes. By the time I'd finished I was famished. I thought about the guy with the lobster.

At the counter Charlemagne folded my chosen items into soft tissue paper and then placed them into a couple of large fancy bags with his shop's name on in fancy lettering: *Charlemagne.*

I liked that name, I really did.

I stood wearing the clothes I had chosen for today – a bottle green rolled neck sweater in a fine cotton, slim-fit navy chinos and oxblood loafers that fitted like a pair of gloves.

I told Charlemagne to get rid of the clothes I'd been wearing and he obliged. I paid with cash, of course, and left with the promise that I'd return, knowing full well that I wouldn't.

Charlemagne waved at me from the window. I waved back and then lit a cigarette, before heading back the way I came, this time more familiar with my surroundings. When I entered the alley it was still buzzing with people, some new crowds but some still the same. I sauntered past the bistro with the orange canopy, stopped and peered in.

The man who'd occupied the window had now gone, his table cleared and re-made. I guessed the time must be around late afternoon. I felt ravenous. Only alcohol and coffee had passed through my lips for the past thirty-six hours. I stepped up to the door and went in.

When the waiter greeted me, I asked if I could have a table by the window. He obliged. The menus were in French and English, in a fancy script. One was a large, single sheet of crisp white paper the size of a good map, the other a small rectangular wine list. I placed them face down on the table as a sign I was ready to order. I knew what I wanted.

The place was still quite full – afternoon lunches turning into social gatherings over good wine. Eventually I was greeted by an oldish woman in a white shirt and black skirt with a white pinny attached. Her grey hair was tied back in a bun. She had no real distinctive features: average greeny-blue eyes and an alright complexion. She had a sense of humbleness about her, a kind woman who'd just done the job for too many years. Her English was weak, my French no better, but we got through the exchange and I believed I'd managed to order a carafe of white wine and the lobster… We would see.

She took away the menus and nearly managed a smile. There were two tables at the front in the bay window – mine and an adjacent one occupied by a

68

young couple, tourists, with big cameras and city maps sprawled out in front of them, scribbled with points of interest. The tables were round and small and only big enough to fit two people – or one large man. He was probably enjoying an espresso now in one of the fancy coffee bars, or a chocolate sundae – one of the ones in the tall glasses that never ended. Probably the latter.

Beside me was a table to fit four people. This was empty. Neatly folded tissues and sparkling glasses, silver cutlery placed with precision, a single bright exotic flower sitting proudly in a slim glass vase. The bistro was narrow; the right-hand wall was covered in black-and-white photos of old movie stars, the bar opposite was mahogany and worn, with four stools, only one occupied.

Between the bar and the wall three rectangular tables had been pushed together, leaving just enough space for a walkway to the back, where a serving hatch and swing door to the kitchen could be found. Six elderly men sat at these tables, grazing multiple wonderful-looking dishes that smelled divine. They were guzzling back red wine from large goblets and spoke loudly through mouthfuls of food. The bartender looked on, a young guy in between jobs, smart black waistcoat and crisp white shirt. He could have been French, but then again, maybe he wasn't. He was drying glasses with a dull expression.

She sat with her back to me nursing a clear short drink, rubbing her finger around the rim – the one occupied stool at the bar. I couldn't see her face.

My wine was brought to the table by a different waitress this time, with skinny legs that went on forever. She was in her forties and scrubbed up well. Same uniform as the woman before but worn far more sexily. Shorter skirt, tighter shirt buttons, undone to show some cleavage. She had good breasts, firm but not fake. I could always tell the difference. She poured the wine and left me alone. I took a sip and it was OK. I turned back to face the bar. The bartender had disappeared. Maybe a cigarette break, maybe his shift was over. She was still there, though, but this time looking directly at me.

She was wearing a black mini dress and stockings and was sitting with her legs crossed. Great legs. She had on patent high heels with red soles, and had no jewellery apart from a man-sized watch. From where I was sitting it appeared to be an Audemars Piguet. I had an eye for expensive watches, even though I couldn't afford them.

I took another sip of my wine. This time it tasted better. Dry, just how I liked it.

Her face seemed young – twenty, twenty-five, I would say. Her thick eyebrows were shaped to perfection; her brown eyes never left mine. Her hair was dark and wavy that appeared effortlessly good. I was transfixed.

I got shy and turned away, playing with the salt- and pepper-pots for a second or two before looking back. She'd also now turned away and was rummaging around in the pockets of the fur coat lying on the stool next to her. She produced a packet of cigarettes and a box of matches. She took a smoke from the packet with her mouth. Her plump lips were painted a bright red that matched the soles of her shoes. She stood up from her stool and glided towards the door. She had a fantastic figure, long and slim. She glanced over and smiled before walking out. From the window I saw her light her cigarette. She was standing with her back to me, legs apart, her left hand on her hip, her right hand holding the cigarette. She took a drag, tilted her head back and blew a cloud of smoke into the air. Fuck, she made smoking sexy. I admired her figure again. Great curves, a peach of an arse.

I found my Marlboro pack and got up, only to be intercepted by the older of the two waitresses – humble, no smile. She was holding a plate out in front of her. My lobster, mouthwatering. I sat back down. I could eat a horse. I think they did in France? The waitress put the plate in front of me and I got stuck in. The best thing about eating alone was you never needed to wait for anyone else's food to arrive before you could begin. I hated having to do that.

The meal was simple but excellently done: a whole lobster garnished with a few herbs, two wedges of lemon and a small pot of melted butter. I cracked through the bright orange-red shell with the neat set of tools provided and sucked on the tender sweet meat within. I savoured every mouthful, took a sip of wine and refilled my glass. I continued to watch her through the window.

She was probably gone for ten minutes, chain-smoking through three cigarettes while making several calls on her phone. When she finally came back in I'd finished my food and had ordered a second carafe of wine, which I said I'd take at the bar. We made eye contact again as she passed me to regain her seat. I smiled and she smiled back. I got up from the table and stepped over to the bar to sit two stools along from her, where my carafe awaited me.

When I glanced across to her, she was staring straight ahead, deep in thought.

Her black stockings had lace at the top. I could see the flesh on her thigh as she sat with her left leg over the right. Fuck, she turned me on so much. I drank some more wine, taking a big glug. Dutch courage and all that. Then I leaned in towards her. Feeling my presence, she turned and faced me, staring deep into my eyes. A shiver run up my spine. For a second, time stood still and I was trapped in the moment.

'Can I buy you a drink?' I said. Cheap line. It's all I had.

There was a pause. Maybe she didn't speak English. Us Brits just assumed everyone else did. But before the silence became awkward, she responded in an accent that wasn't French and one I didn't recognise.

'Vodka, just ice. Thank you,' she said, in a soft voice.

I signalled to the bartender but he was already on it. He assumed it was a double and I watched him pour a big splash of Cîroc into a fresh glass, over ice.

He placed the drink in front of her under a new coaster and took away her empty.

'I will add to your bill, sir,' he said.

'Thank you,' I said, without taking my eyes off of her.

She raised her glass. 'Cheers.' Then she tapped the stool next to hers with a manicured hand. 'Join me?'

I was like a blind man who'd regained his sight on Monday and was told he'd won the lottery on Tuesday. I picked up my wine and moved across.

As I nestled into my seat, she introduced herself formally as Zenith Provoski. I introduced myself in turn with a cock-and-bull story about being a big-time FX trader in town for a couple of days on business. She bought it. Of course she would. Why wouldn't she?

Zenith told me she was from Ukraine but not much else. The conversation was always more about me. She was a good listener and I liked that. I enjoyed talking about myself, a completely fabricated tale that even I was starting to believe.

An hour became two and two became three. We chatted into the night without a care in the world. The drinks flowed. Zenith was more than generous in paying her own way. I liked that in a woman. She didn't say much, but when she did she spoke with a fine intelligence, a maturity beyond her young years. She had this great smile, a glimmer of teeth, revealing a smidgin of coquetry.

People came and people left, afternoon turned to evening and evening became the end of the night. The staff were beginning to put chairs on tables as I peered round the now empty establishment. The bartender appeared tired and bored. He'd been wiping the same glass now for over ten minutes. It wouldn't be long before they asked us to leave. I wondered where she lived.

'I'm staying at the Royal,' I said. 'Would you care to join me for a drink there?'

I thought about Azurine and the story that my wife had gone on to Disneyland with my kids. It wouldn't look good, me entering the hotel with another woman. I glanced at the clock behind the bar. 11:15 pm. Azurine would have finished her shift by now though. In her place a night porter who wouldn't give a shit.

I waited for Zenith's response. She took her time, finished her drink, then began to paint her lips. The delay was agonising. The longer it went on, the longer I felt it was just not going to happen. Had I read the signs wrong? Had I spent the last five hours wasting my time here?

For Christ's sake, say something!

She put her lipstick back into a smart clutch bag then took both my hands in hers. I went cold.

'I have an apartment a few blocks from here. How about we go there?'

I felt a rush of adrenaline erupt inside my body. My penis had burst out, it was rock hard.

I composed myself. I'm sure she could feel the sexual tension in my body through the palms of my hands she was now gently rubbing.

Eventually I said, 'OK, great.' A man of many words I thought, but fuck it. I'd done my talking. I'd sealed the fucking deal. I looked at her freshly glossed lips and imagined them kissing my groin. I glanced down at her legs and imagined them wrapped around me. I thought of her breasts in my mouth. I fantasised about being deep inside her.

She stood and flung her fur coat over her shoulders like a model, real Irina Shayk-like. She moved in close to me. The first kiss of many, I thought, but instead she whispered into my ear.

'One thousand Euro for the whole night.'

7

I left her at the bar without an answer. I said I just needed to go to the toilet.

The men's was in the corner of the bistro. One urinal and one cubicle, a small sink with a tap that dripped beneath a square mirror with a crack running through its centre. The walls were tiled, though some were missing. A single light bulb flickered above my head, giving off a dull light. The strong potent smell of chemicals from the deodoriser blocks placed in the urinal tarnished the air. It was damp and dingy.

I went over to the mirror and stared at my faint reflection. My eyes were red and my skin was pale. I rested both my hands on the sink, took a deep breath and thought about the proposition just presented to me.

Dirty fucking whore. Dirty fucking whore. The words spun around inside my head in big neon capital letters, all singing, all dancing, flashing away like the entrance to a Vegas casino.

I clenched my fists and stared deep and close into my reflection. The moisture from my breath steamed the glass.

'Dirty fucking whore. Dirty fucking whore!'

I was screaming at the top of my voice. I was surprised no one heard. Maybe they were all waiting for me outside the restaurant, the workforce waiting to lock up, the whore waiting for her next pay cheque, all of them smoking in a discreet circle, laughing about the man they'd left behind. Yes, I bet all the staff knew. I bet she had a nice little arrangement with the owner, paying him regular instalments of hush money so she could use his premises as a pick-up joint and get her clientèle to run up huge bar bills as part of the bargain. The slut.

I'd fallen for her hook, line and sinker, drawn in by her beauty and innocent charm, taken in by her soft voice and intellectual chat, in awe of her sophisticated style.

I only knew one type of prostitute: haggard faces and ill-fitting clothes, the smell of bad perfume, the taste of cheap tobacco, desperate ladies of the night seeking cash for their next score. Contaminated bitches infected with a mass of disease. The dirt off your shoe, the promiscuous tramp off a suburban street corner, working it for the flow of kerb-crawlers desperate for an easy lay.

Dinah Washington once sang 'What a Difference a Day Makes'. The words spun around in my head. What else could happen in this twenty-four hours? Five minutes ago I was the guy at the bar with the bombshell, the sex on legs, the fucking crème de la crème. Five minutes ago I had the testosterone of Eros, the confidence of Casanova, the invincibility of the fucking Roman Empire. I thought they were all looking on in envy, the men wanting to be with her, the women wanting to be her.

Five minutes ago I'd forgotten who I was and what I'd done. Five minutes ago I felt normal again.

What a difference five minutes make.

Yes, I bet they all knew – the waitress with the legs, the humble sixty-something-year-old, the bartender and the six local men who dined for an age. I bet they were all laughing behind my back, snide remarks in their native tongue.

It all made sense now – the watch, the fur coat, the unmarked Louboutin's, bought by guys who could all stick their dicks in her at will if they paid the right price.

'Fucking whore,' I screamed again, my saliva spraying the mirror.

I composed myself. I needed to get a grip. Drinking heavily on the antidepressants sent me insane. I splashed my face with freezing cold water from the decrepit tap laced with limescale. I desperately needed a smoke.

I patted my face down with a hard towel from one of those old, unhygienic dispensers you rarely see anymore.

Good job the food was great in here as this place wasn't winning any awards for the toilets.

I took a deep breath and one final look at my reflection in the cracked mirror. I didn't recognise the man staring back at me.

She was still sitting at the bar, legs crossed, looking as good as when I left her.

I approached and she smiled – the same smile she'd given me five hours ago. The staff had left and the bartender was juggling a huge set of keys. He had his coat on, a blue quilted Barbour-style riding jacket fastened right into his neck, ready to face the cool night air.

I picked up my Marlboros and lighter up from the bar. The lighter was a silver Zippo engraved with my late granddad's initials. It reminded me of a happier time, me and Gramps sneaking off to the betting shop to indulge in his only sins, the gee-gees and smoking – both of which my nan didn't approve.

I put a fag to my lips and said, 'Let's smoke,' before collecting my bags from under the table where I'd previously sat at alone. Two fancy bags with neat string handles, the garments inside folded to perfection and laced with fine tissue paper by the delicate hands of Charlemagne. I thought about him for a second, his beautiful shop and nice manners. I liked the person I was with him, the man I knew I could have been, the man deep down I wanted to be. But there was a switch – oh, sweet Jesus, there was a switch, and when it was flicked it was flicked, from Jekyll to Hyde within a heartbeat.

I thought about the guy at the station, as wide as he was tall. I wondered how he was doing. I'd never taken anything that far before. Would I go further? Would I? Could I?

I was sensing more this time – a deep inner thought that danced around my head with clogs on. Bang. Bang. Bang. It wouldn't go away.

Would I have actually killed him given the chance?

Bang. Bang. Bang. There it was again. The next stage, murder, stomping its feet like a petulant child.

Would I? Would I actually go through with it?

What a difference a day makes.

8

Outside the air was cool. No, freezing, in fact. A fine sleet cut diagonally through the dark Paris night, its path to the cobbled streets illuminated by the rows of street lamps. I smoked, so did she. We stood under the canopy to avoid the weather.

The bartender locked up behind us and disappeared into the night. We both watched him walk into the darkness until he was a speck in the distance. Jesus, it was cold. Maybe I would see Charlemagne again for a decent winter coat. I looked over at her. She seemed snug in her fur. I wanted to get inside with her and feel the warmth of her amazing body.

I wondered how such a great-looking girl could end up a hooker. She could have been a model. I mean, she was in the right city for it. I'd read somewhere once that Coco Chanel once said: 'A girl should be two things: classy and fabulous.' I didn't recall the next sentence containing the word 'slut'.

We hadn't spoken for about two minutes. That awkward silence when two relative strangers have run out of things to say. I broke the deadlock with a reply to her statement over ten minutes ago.

'One thousand Euro for the whole night?'

'The whole night,' she said, and took a deep drag on her cigarette.

I chucked my drained butt into the gutter. 'For a thousand Euro I want to be able to do anything to you.'

There was a slight pause before her response, but then she moved in right close and whispered in my ear, 'Anything.'

9

We walked through dark narrow back streets that were shadowed with white-bricked two-up-and-two-downs and intertwined the cobbled streets deep into the heart of the city. We passed churches from another century, towering steeples spiralling and vanishing into the dreary night sky above us. The sleet still fell, riding horizontally on a strong, cold, northerly wind that hit us hard.

We didn't speak much, just the occasional glance followed by a false smile. There was no more need for either of us to play the game. The deal had been struck. No pretence, just a formality.

We eventually arrived at a wooden door that could have easily been black. The only reason I knew the colour is that she told me.

'Here we are, blue door,' she said, as she searched in her clutch bag. She scrambled around for several seconds before pulling out a single key, which she put in the door. With a slight bit of force it opened to reveal a steep set of stairs that disappeared into the darkness.

The weather was a joke. I was wet through and eager to get in, but as I made to pass the threshold she stuck her arm across the door and looked me straight in the eye.

'A thousand Euro. Please wire to these details.'

She shoved her phone in my face. A sort code and a security number glowed back at me.

'I have cash'

'*Encore mieux.*'

I handed over the money. I didn't have much left after shopping and lunch. It was going quick, but I didn't care. They could catch me tomorrow. I had another three nights in the Royal and just over three grand in the safe. Once the cash had gone, who knew? I'd worry about that then.

She put the money in her bag, removed her arm from the door and told me to walk to the top of the stairs, which I did. I eventually reached a small landing with two doors either side. We approached the one to the left. I stepped to one side and she opened the door. We entered into a reasonably sized square room lit by a stylish arc floor-lamp in the corner. She took off her coat and threw it onto a red leather sofa that had been placed against the back, white-brick wall.

Above the sofa was a shelf scattered with oval photo frames all featuring the same woman over a generation.

Her mother, I guessed. The shelf was about a foot wide. Beyond it were tall, old-fashioned shuttered windows, stretching to the top of the high ceiling, that looked down onto the street we'd just been in.

It felt good to be out of the cold, hard sleet.

The rest of the room was quite bare, but less was more and all that. A glass coffee table stacked with several editions of *Vogue* deliberately spread out like a deck of cards. The wall adjacent to the sofa was again white-brick but had no windows. A stud wall, it would have been an ideal place to hang a TV, but instead there was a bookshelf stacked to the brim with literature. There were books on travel and art. There were stories by Hemingway and HG Wells.

Tucked away in the corner of the room was a rocking chair stained white, where the arc floor-lamp was strategically placed to create a great reading space. I stood by the front door feeling the effect of the drink. The night air had not been kind. I was unsteady on my feet and swayed ever so slightly from side to side.

'Drink?' she said.

'I'm fine.' The clock was ticking and I was a thousand Euro down. I wanted to get started, get down to business. Everything.

'OK. Come with me.'

She walked across the apartment to a door and opened

it, signalling for me to follow with her finger. I did.

It was dark inside, just the light from the other room creating new shadows. I stood, I waited.

She lit two long candles that stood in what looked like a marble fireplace and told me to shut the door. I did.

The flames flickered as she moved across what I could now see was a bedroom as the dark shadows came to life under their soft orange glow.

The room was simple from what I could see in the candlelight. Three brick walls, one of which was half-wall, half long sash windows. Their wooden shutters were tilted open. I could see the tops of the street lights outside, their glow exaggerating the drops of slushy falling sleet. The last wall was completely covered with a built-in wardrobe. I imagined the rails of slutty outfits vying for her attention. There was a large bed with a wrought-iron headboard backed against the wall with the windows. I wondered how many before me had been cuffed to it? There wasn't much other furniture – a nightstand buried under a hoard of perfume bottles, a large rectangle mirror above it that reflected the flickering candle flames.

She moved round to the foot of the bed and gestured for me to come over. I did.

I got about within three feet of her and she put her hand out for me to stop. I did.

She rolled her dress over the tops of her slender shoulders and it fell to the floor. She took off her bra and then rolled her thong down across her thighs and also let it drop. Her stomach was flat and toned, her skin was golden and glistened in the faint candlelight. Her breasts were small but perfect. Her cunt was bald.

She sat on the edge of the bed. 'Your turn.'

I got out of my wet clothes faster than Harry Houdini from a straitjacket. I moved to the edge of the bed where she still sat. She opened her mouth and swallowed my dick.

We fucked for the next two hours in between fags and sips of vodka. I was OK. She was out of this world and like nothing I had ever had. Everything and more. We carried on into the night, taking coke to keep us going, her supply as plentiful as sugar.

At 2:15 am she said I needed to go. She had a flight to catch at ten, some business in Zurich or something. A rich businessman ready to part with his thousand Euros no doubt. I didn't mind, I was spent. Well, almost. I asked if we could do it one more time. She agreed and I got on top.

I fucked her like it was my last time. Maybe it would be. I was forceful. She liked my hands around her neck. We got into in, like before. She liked to make out I was raping her. She screamed for me to get off her, part of the game, part of the thrill.

Sex on cocaine was the best. It made sex longer and harder, it made orgasms more intense. It made us do things we wouldn't usually do.

I started to add more force and began to dig my thumbs hard into her windpipe. She began to fight for her breath.

'Too much. Too much. Please, you're hurting me,' she gasped.

I carried on, no intention of stopping, the coke fizzing through my bloodstream, driving me on. She began to struggle hard, wriggling like a giant eel, but I was far too strong. My full bodyweight was driving through into the palms of the hands locked around her neck like a nut tightened around a screw. She knew now it was no longer a game. She knew now that I was trying to kill her.

I increased the pressure. She started to choke, her face red, her eyes rolling to the back of her head. She kept fighting, everything she had, twisting and turning vigorously to escape my hold. It was indeed a remarkable display of defiance and I would have been bitterly disappointed if she'd shown anything less. I enjoyed the struggle immensely.

I added more force. I could feel the bones in her neck between my fingers, I could smell the vodka on her breath as she hopelessly fought for breath, for life.

She dug her nails deep into my side, drawing blood. The pain felt remarkably good. I hoped it would scar, a constant reminder of my first victim. Would it be my last? Would it?

It went quiet. Nothing but the sleet again, tapping against the windowpanes. There was a stillness in the air, like the whole world had just stopped for a few seconds. I imagined cars outside that had been moving now frozen in the road, second hands no longer ticking, travelling clouds now motionless, like sleeping sheep in a field.

I looked down at her, my hands still locked around her neck. She seemed peaceful, a dreamlike daze. I removed my hands and her head fell limply away to the side.

It was as if a switch had been flicked in my head, and my brain was a steel pressure cooker with one dial and three settings: sane, insane and fucking psychopath.

I realised my dick was still inside, still hard. I fucked her one more time, without the struggle. That dial was switched to the psychopath setting, for sure.

10

I got dressed standing over her body, I wondered how long it would take before her rotten flesh would begin to smell. This was all new to me and I had definitely not thought things through.

My prints would be all over the flat, all over her. My semen would be inside her.

My clothes were still damp. Then I remembered the new ones, so I stripped down again, got out of the bedroom and found my fancy bags, stacked by the front door.

The light in the room was mellow, just a glow from the lamp in the corner. I picked out a pair of grey trousers that could have been black. I put on a purple V-neck sweater that could have been brown. Colour combinations, considering the circumstances, were irrelevant. The main thing was they weren't wet. The dry clothes against my skin felt good.

I went back into the bedroom. She was lying on the

bed looking like she'd awaken at any minute. I scoped the room and found her watch, the Audemars, on the side. I put it on. It was 2:35 am. I began rifling through an array of drawers, not sure what I was looking for. There was a small chest that only contained fine lingerie. I took a pair of French knickers and inhaled deep into the crotch. They smelled good. I put them in my pocket as a small souvenir.

I opened up the fitted wardrobe, which was full to the brim. *Rails of slutty outfits vying for her attention.* At the bottom were a dozen or more shoeboxes, stacked on top of one another, splashed in print spelling out designer labels: Jimmy Choo, Vera Wang and Christian Louboutin, Dior, Manolo Blahnik and Yves Saint Laurent. I flipped the lids and searched through the boxes like a desperate madman to find nothing but tissue paper and killer heels.

I began to feel myself getting angry. I needed to get out of here.

Penny was often black-and-blue. There was one time I beat her so badly, she didn't leave the house for three weeks while waiting for the bruising to go down. She always gave me another chance. My dear Penny. I wondered what she was doing now.

I needed to get the fuck out of the apartment. I'd never experienced the pungent smell of death before and didn't want to start tonight. I once read that the smell of a decomposing body was a stomach-churning, sickly odour like nothing else in this world. I'd left the freezer door open one morning without realising. When I returned from work the stench of rotting meat knocked me back. A decomposing human body was meant to be a million times worse.

I kept looking. A thousand-Euro-a-night hooker had to have a stash of cash somewhere. I searched the back of the wardrobe with a desperate hand. Nothing. Maybe times have changed. A hooker who charged so much and lived in such a lush apartment probably had a bank account – all her money locked away in a high-interest Geneva deposit fund. I then remembered how earlier in the night she'd shown me the account details to wire the money to. Fuck. But then I thought about it again. A large proportion of her clients would have been married men for sure, or at least have a girlfriend in tow. They couldn't be seen to be wiring money, leaving a trace. No, these guys would definitely pay cash. Now a thousand-Euro-a-night hooker would soon accumulate a fair bit of cash from this discreet clan. A fair bit, indeed. Of course there was nothing stopping her banking this bread, but she'd do it every so often, once it had built up a bit. That surely meant there was a stash somewhere. But what if she had already banked it? Built up a nice bit of collateral and paid it in just recently? Could my timing be so inopportune?

I slammed my fist down onto the floor of the wardrobe in frustration, dislodging one of the wooden panels at the base.

The base was made up of around a dozen slim panels, around six to eight inches in length. They weren't fixed, just slotted together by a locking system. I removed the panel I'd dislodged and in doing so knocked something from the inner wall. A small chisel that had been masked there, the tape still stuck around the worn wooden handle.

I felt a rush of excitement. A tool deliberately placed could only mean one thing: the panels were often removed. I leaned into the enclosed space and began removing the pieces of wood one by one, starting at the back and making my way to the front. On my hands and knees I felt like an archaeologist unearthing his latest find. Hell, yeah, I was fucking Indiana Jones. Any minute now a gust of cold air would hit my face as I discovered the secret tunnel that led to fortune and glory. OK, not quite, but there was a hole in the floor, no more than a foot deep. It could have been less. There was a gap between the joists and the ceiling of the apartment below.

I lay on my stomach and edged into the darkness. It was damp, and the dust made me sneeze. With my left arm supporting me on one of the joists I rummaged between the wooden beams with my right hand. I estimated six joists in total, running horizontal to me. The first three gaps were empty. I started to think my imagination must have run away with me. Maybe the chisel was there as protection against a certain clientèle that took things too far, a sick pervert who wanted to act out his darkest fantasies.

I thought of that guy. In my head he was vastly overweight, bald and ugly. He would sweat a lot, wear bad shirts but plenty of money, no real friends, just associates. He was arrogant and dishonest, a virgin until he realised you could pay for sex.

I was the polar opposite to him. Wasn't I?

Yes, I was, I was. I definitely was. But I was a killer now, a cold-blooded killer. Fuck, that made me worse! I considered right there and then forgetting the money, getting the hell out and getting back home, confessing about everything and paying the price. I considered it, but then the switch in my head flicked again.

I continued looking.

I was getting hot, frustrated. My left arm was numb from the weight I was putting on it. The closet smelled of her, Chanel No 5. Penny's favourite. I ran my right hand up and down in the fourth gap, same process of elimination as the previous three. Nothing. I edged back, my left arm now plagued with pins and needles. I put my hand into the penultimate space without any conviction, an unconvincing swoop that lacked the scrupulousness of the previous searches. I was now convinced the chisel's sole purpose in life was to stab the temple of the paying guest who wouldn't take no for an answer. It could have been me.

I skimmed the edges hastily, my mind no longer on the job but on getting out of the apartment before dawn broke. I had the watch, it would get me a couple of thousand from a back-street pawnbroker who wouldn't ask any questions. He'd get a bargain and I'd buy myself a few more days.

When I felt it, my heart stopped. A box of some sort, possibly a shoebox just like the many others. But unlike them this was hidden, and hidden well. I grasped it with both hands and pulled it out and into the room. It was a shoebox, but not pretty and shiny and covered in fancy logos like the others. It was plain, old and covered in dust, the edges crumpled. I took a deep breath and removed the lid. I could still hear the sleet driving at the windows. It had got heavier, and it was all I heard, apart from my breathing, rattling through my lungs like the thirty-a-day smoker I'd become.

Inside, it was fucking amazing. I stared for a while with a crooked smile, licked my lips, then scrambled for a cigarette. I planted one in my mouth, sparked a flame and dragged heavily on the butt. A cloud of smoke hung in the air. I brushed it aside and continued to look at the contents of the box. It was beautiful.

When I was ready to leave I glanced down at the bed one more time and at her body. She still looked good, just sleeping.

I imagined how it would be if she wasn't found for weeks, her skin tone marbled, her face bloated. She would be covered in blisters as the body continued to putrefy, fingernails sunk back into the fingers, loss of hair, fluids draining from her mouth and nose as her insides began to decay.

I imagined if she was never found, rotting away ungracefully, her corpse open to the elements, not sealed away in a wooden box where her decline would be private and dignified. There would be no headstone engraved with a lachrymose inscription, no service and no passing words. There would be no gathering of black veils and dark suits, with people congregating in tight groups, telling wonderful stories of the deceased in between tipples of good wine and well-presented canapés.

No laughter, no pain. A life not celebrated, just forgotten.

I thought of her in years to come, still there lying in that same position on the bed, an unrecognisable skeleton, the last pieces of remaining flesh hanging on desperately to the bundle of bones that had replaced a human being. I felt sad, but only for a minute.

I lay down at the end of the bed. I was exhausted. I closed my eyes for what was meant to be only a brief few seconds. I woke up three hours later.

11

The hotel lobby was extremely busy considering it was now 6:45 am. An elderly black guy was waxing the floors with a large machine, whistling an upbeat tune that was drowned out by the hum of his mechanical device. Chambermaids scuttled in and out of my path their hands piled with fresh folded sheets smelling of summer. A young maid was arranging fresh flowers in tall, slim vases. A bellboy in a gleaming uniform was struggling with a luggage cart stacked with Louis Vuitton suitcases and, no doubt, the belongings of the glam fifty-odd-year-old couple who'd stepped out of the stretch on my way in.

I approached the reception desk. Azurine had been replaced with a balding, middle-aged gentleman who wasn't as easy on the eye. He was smart, however. Hotel policy and all that. He was wearing thin-rimmed cat-eye glasses that suited his face, and was cleanly shaven. His thinning thatch was swept from left to right, the hair around the sides, four inches in length, I guess, slicked down with gel. His hair was mainly black, with the odd strand of grey. It shone under the light of the grand chandelier that hung above us. He was drinking what looked like some sort of fruit tea from a posh cup and saucer while shuffling through what seemed to be a batch of invoices. I envied his freshness. I felt like shit. He eyed me up and down as I got closer. I must have looked like shit as well. His eyes were green. They peered out from behind his glasses, watching my every move.

My eyes were red. They felt heavy and sore. I could have done without polite conversation, but I could tell by his body language he was eager for it.

'*Bonjour, monsieur,*' he said, like I was the first person he'd spoken to in days.

'*Bonjour,*' I replied, with slightly less zest.

'You are staying at the hotel, sir?'

'*Oui, oui.*' I confirmed my name and room number and mentioned that I'd had a heavy night. He folded his arms and leaned on the counter, looking like he had a thousand questions.

Lucky for me the glam fifty-something-year-old couple had stepped up to the counter to check in. I moved back for them, for which they were grateful. They were both well-tanned and impeccably dressed. She had a great figure for her age; she was wearing tight white jeans and had a great arse. She had on a white polo top, with a jumper draped over her shoulders, and was holding a Louis Vuitton bag – the same recognisable pattern as the luggage. I noticed her watch was a Cartier.

He was tall, dark and slim, slicked-back grey hair and piercing eyes. He was wearing a sports jacket with dark jeans, and a pale pink shirt with the top three buttons undone.

I didn't notice much chemistry between them. He did the talking, in good French, and she stood back checking her smartphone, the world at her manicured fingertips.

I took my opportunity and made a quick exit towards the lifts. When I turned round one more time to check out her arse, she glanced up and smiled at me. Caught red-handed. I smiled back, embarrassed.

Seconds later I was travelling vertically, the same lift as previously, before the shit got real. Well, the current shit, at least. London was a fog.

One minute later I was back in my room. I chucked everything on the floor, including what I was wearing, took off the watch and put it in the safe along with the box. Then I drew the curtains and got into bed. I thought about ordering room service but changed my mind. Instead, I'd sleep until noon then go out to lunch, somewhere posh and exclusive.

I turned my thoughts back to Penny. How was she

coping? Had she reported me missing yet, or had the police already tracked me back to her? They might be with her now, grilling her, intimidating her, going over every aspect of my life for reasons why I'd done what I did. Maybe they thought she was in on it, hiding me away somewhere, like some sort of fugitive. Maybe they were one step further, picking me up on CCTV boarding the Eurostar. Maybe the French police were already looking for me, hot on my heels, tracing me back to this hotel. They could be talking to the reception desk right now, a bunch of officers packing out the lobby, tossing my photos about like confetti.

'Dans quelle chambre habite cet homme?'

I switched off the lights and closed my eyes. If they came, they came. Hopefully it would be in the dead of night, my foggy, half-awake grasp of the situation diluting reality.

I thought about better things. The restaurant for lunch. Grand ceilings and mirrored walls, white tablecloths and fine silver cutlery. Tall, leather-bound menus and crystal glasses, soft music playing in the background, ivory keys and delicate fingers. The food exquisite, the wine even better.

12

I was awoken by a conversation in the corridor outside, two chambermaids chewing the fat in French. I really should have paid more attention in Miss White's language classes, instead of staring at her great breasts. She used to wear one of those large jumpers that hung off the shoulder, revealing her bra strap. She must have been early thirties at the time, petite body but huge fucking tits. I think I spent half my school years locked away in a toilet cubicle masturbating over her, which probably explained my pathetic grades and constantly sore dick.

I rolled out of bed and opened the curtains. A blinding light attacked the darkness, making me squint for several seconds until my eyes adjusted to the new day. Outside, the sky across Paris was a brilliant blue, without a single cloud. The sun was shining at its highest point, everything below glistening in its rays.

I opened the window. The air was crisp. I lit my morning fix and watched the city below go about its business in between deep drags.

After my smoke I took a shower. It felt great. Really hot. I washed my hair with the complimentary shampoo and lathered my body with a citrus-smelling body-wash. Afterwards, I chose a black cashmere cardigan and a white Oxford shirt, with a light grey pair of cotton trousers in a slim fit and plain black loafers. I finished off the look with a single-breasted sports jacket in fine dogtooth. It was made of pure wool and would take the chill off this January afternoon. It was January wasn't it? What day was it even? I didn't care. My stomach told me it was lunchtime and that was all that mattered.

I opened the safe. Inside was the Audemars. For a second or two I stared at it blankly, like I'd forgotten. Like last night may have been just a nightmare.

I put the watch on and then pulled out the shoebox and took the lid off. Inside was a bundle of used notes. I poured the contents onto the bed and began to flick through them. There was even more than I'd first thought. At a guess I estimated twenty thousand, maybe more. Mainly large bills, 50 Euro notes and upwards. It took me over ten minutes to count it all. I was way out. Over 30,000.

I put 5,000 Euro in my jacket pocket and returned the rest to the safe, then checked the watch. 1 pm precisely. I was famished.

I caught a glimpse of myself in the glass door of the wardrobe. I looked good; I felt even better. Putting yesterday to the back of my mind, I left the suite with surprising optimism as I set foot into a new day.

The lift stopped at the second floor – the lady from this morning, the elegant fifty-something-year-old, this time alone. She stepped in and smiled. I smiled back, blushing, thinking back to our last encounter.

She looked fucking amazing, in a white leather mini skirt and knee-high black boots. She was also wearing a tight white shirt and a very-expensive-looking silk jacket in olive green, with a distinctive oriental pattern running through it. Her hair was tied back and her make-up done to perfection.

'Going anywhere nice?' I said, making small talk.

'For lunch,' she replied, in an American accent.

'With your husband?'

She seemed a little confused. 'My husband?'

'My apologies. I thought the guy you were checking in with this morning was your husband, no?'

'My brother.'

We reached the ground floor and stepped out into the lobby. There was no sign of the Police Nationale.

'Sorry, I just presumed he was your husband.'

'No apologies needed. The usual assumption.'

'So, lunch with your brother?'

'No, he flew back to the States after checking me in this morning. I'm here alone for five days.'

'Business?'

'Just pleasure. And yourself?'

'Business, unfortunately. I have an investor here in Paris.' More bullshit.

'Alone?'

'Yes.'

'Where are you off to now?'

'Lunch.'

'Business or pleasure?'

'Pleasure.'

'Care to join me instead? Be nice to have some company.'

'That would be lovely.'

And just like that we walked out of the hotel and into the winter sun.

13

The Jules Verne restaurant on the second floor of the Eiffel Tower offered exceptional dining, she had told me, with exquisite views of Paris. Who was I to argue?

Her chauffer picked us up from outside the hotel, and we entered the restaurant at 1:35 pm. The establishment was heaving. I couldn't see a spare table as we approached the maître d'. The place smelled fucking great – whiffs of this whiffs of that, an intoxicating heaven. I watched a bartender pour something over ice with steady hands, and waiters done up like penguins ducking in and out of tables, carrying trays filled with plates of food and drink. They weaved around each over with a ceaseless ease, masters of their trade, the best in the business. I took in the clientèle, couples and groups all soaking up the warming ambience. I couldn't wait to join them. That's if we got a table. Please God, let us get a table.

The maître d' was on the phone but cut his conversation short when he saw us approaching. He was all smiles, big white teeth framed by a grey well-groomed goatee beard. His hair was fine and cropped, with long sideburns. His complexion was dark and sun-kissed, like he'd just arrived back from an exotic holiday. He came out from behind his stand and greeted Priscilla, with a warm cuddle and two extravagant kisses to each cheek.

'Priscilla, darling, what a wonderful surprise,' he said, in a strong French accent.

Priscilla Hugh-Garcia. The surname had rung a bell when she'd told me it on the steps of the hotel.

' And who do we have here, darling?' The maître d' looked me up and down, his hand on his chin.

'This is Will Lindeman, a friend of mine.'

The real Will Lindeman was an ex-colleague of mine. It was the first name that had come into my head.

'A pleasure to meet you, Mr Lindeman.' He reached out and we shook hands. His hands were soft and his handshake weak. I noticed his fingernails were extremely groomed and seemed to be glossed with a clear varnish.

'Léon Moreau,' he introduced himself, before throwing himself all over Priscilla again. They chatted away like old friends. Smalltalk, usual stuff. You're looking well, it's been too long, how's the family, something about his mum turning eighty.

I stood in the foreground and took in the restaurant again. It was a good-sized area with tall windows letting natural daylight pour through. The furnishings were contemporary and elegant, crisp white tablecloths just how I imagined them. I wondered where we would sit, as I could still not see a spare table. I was soon to find out.

The maître d', whose name I'd already forgotten, stepped away from the brisk conversation with Priscilla and signalled over a waiter by clicking his fingers arrogantly.

As the young man approached, the maître d' straightened his tie to the guy's embarrassment.

'Miss Hugh-Garcia's usual table,' he said.

The waiter disappeared for a few seconds before reappearing with a small round table on his shoulder. He began to walk through the restaurant and Priscilla signalled for me to follow. I did, watching her every curve.

The young waiter placed the table by the window, even getting the tables either side to move back slightly to give us space. Next thing there were staff all around us, setting our places. I felt like a fucking movie star. People nearby stared at us. I loved the attention.

We sat down. Paris with a view to kill for. I gazed down at the city beneath us, so far away it looked like a model. Tiny cars the size of my fingernails, people like insects. It reminded me of the poster from the coffee house, *Attack of the 50 Foot Woman*. London, yesterday.

It seemed like a lifetime ago.

My dreamy gaze was broken as a waitress approached the table with a bottle of champagne, which I didn't recall Priscilla ordering.

'I hope you don't mind, but I don't drink anything else here, and they know that,' she said.

'Not at all.' I checked the label on the bottle. Krug '98.

We began to sip from our cut-glass champagne flutes, looking deep into each other's eyes, trying to suss each other out. Strangers in a foreign country brought together by unique circumstances, now having an intimate lunch.

'Hugh-Garcia, as in the oil company?' I asked, breaking the tension. The name had come back to me.

'You got me.'

That explained the drawl in her accent. Texan.

She explained her father was indeed William Hugh-Garcia, the billionaire Texan oil tycoon. She went on to say that he'd only recently died of a heart attack.

'I'm sorry to hear that.'

'Don't be. We were never close. My brother was always the apple of his eye.'

'Is it just the two of you?'

'Yes, we're twins. My mother died immediately after giving birth to us.'

'That's terrible.'

'Hard to grieve after someone you've never met.'

'But still, it must have been hard not having a mother, ever.'

'Shit happens.' She took a drop of her drink. So did I. The champagne was good. 'The way I look at it,' she said, 'is there's always someone worse off. Until the age of ten I was brought up by a nanny. A nice woman. Unprivileged families don't get that luxury, do they?'

'I guess not. Do you mind me asking why you and your father weren't close?'

'It's like he blamed me for my mother's death. Apparently, if we hadn't been twins she would have survived.'

'But why just you? Why not your brother, as well?'

'He only ever wanted a boy. Told me that once after a few bourbons. Nice thing to hear.' She took a mouthful of her drink – a big fucking glug, like it was easing the pain. 'He wanted a son to run his empire. I was just an inconvenience, the runt of the litter.'

'So what happened after the age of ten?' I said, thinking how the fuck did this conversation get so deep so soon. Maybe it helped her talking about it to a near stranger. A sort of therapy. I was happy to oblige, sit back, listen and drink champagne.

'I was shipped off to boarding school for the next six years. I then spent three years travelling, to find

111

myself. All funded, of course, as it meant I was out of the picture. And then on my return I got given a hefty allowance and a New York apartment, and that's been my life ever since.'

'What about your brother?'

'We are close. He went into the family business, of course, but always came to visit me. A few times I went off the rails. Alcohol, drug addiction – the usual rich kid cliché. He always helped me through, stayed with me when times were rough. He always said Dad had asked after me, but I know he just said that to make me feel better. He never really gave a fuck. His whole life he just threw money at me to stay out of his way.'

Only ten minutes had passed since we'd sat down and already I knew so much. I'd only expected to find out her favourite place to go on holiday, or what she liked doing in her spare time. I continued to probe and listen, though. It made me forget about my troubles, hearing someone else's. For now, anyway.

'So what next?' I asked, enthusiastically.

'Next?' she repeated, with a puzzled expression.

'Now that he's dead.'

'Oh, right. Well, that's the whole reason I'm here.' She took a small mirror out of her bag and checked her make-up. She looked fine from where I was sitting. 'My brother has laid this whole trip on,' she said, still looking in the mirror.

'Why Paris?'

'Basically it's to keep me well out of the States while he ties up the estate. He can then go on to bullshit me that my father left me stuff in the will. He'll then give me a portion of his share and at the same time lead me to believe that our dad actually gave a shit. It's sweet. He loved his dad dearly and would always defend his actions, but I'm well past caring what he ever thought of me. As long as I get my share, I don't give a fuck, and will play along with this whole pathetic game.'

She sounded bitter, like the cards life had dealt her would have her folding at the first opportunity. I would have taken her hand over mine any day of the week.

'You obviously come here often,' I said. 'Judging by the reception and treatment you got here today.'

'Only three or four times a year but money talks, right? And the Hugh-Garcia name opens many doors. I love to shop and my brother has a couple of business interests out here.'

'Real estate?'

'No, he owns a couple of casinos. One on the French Riviera and one right here in Paris – the Red and Black Club. It's only two blocks from the Royal Hotel.'

Yes, the Red and Black Club. I remembered passing it last night.

'Yes, I know it,' I said. 'Lovely place. I was there last night. That's where I was coming back from when I saw you and your brother this morning.'

'Casinos – I can't stand them myself. Never got the whole Vegas thing. You win anything?'

'I did, as a matter of fact. About thirty thousand.'

14

The pan-seared duck starter was astounding, the tender ox cheek for mains even better. Champagne had helped the conversation flow, too. Dessert had long passed, but I could still taste the honey-roasted pear ice cream on my lips. We were now enjoying liqueurs in front of a tranquil sunset.

We'd spoken about moving on. Priscilla had mentioned a members' only bar that sounded right up my street. I footed the bill, despite her protests, and she finally gave up when I said it was technically her brother's money anyway, after my casino win. She laughed out loud and champagne came out of her nose. Then we both laughed at that. She called her chauffeur and advised that we'd be down in five minutes, enough time for me to take a leak.

Priscilla said she'd wait for me downstairs as she was desperate for a smoke. She asked for a light and I chucked her some matches I'd picked up in the hotel earlier. I had left my granddad's engraved Zippo back in the hotel safe, I wasn't going to risk going forward losing the only thing that meant something to me.

I made my way to the toilet. The restaurant had thinned out. That time between lunch and dinner.

The toilet was empty apart from a middle-aged man with long grey hair and a moustache that curled at the ends. He was wearing a bubble-gum pink blazer with large brass buttons, a white shirt and a black velvet bow tie. He was standing by the sink with a well-ordered array of aftershaves and neatly folded hand towels, and a small silver plate filled with loose change. I hated these guys. I was perfectly able to dry my own hands, without needing to pay someone to hand me the fucking tissue. We made eye contact and he greeted me with a real Pan Am smile. I managed a half-smile. No teeth – more of a smirk. I used the urinal, pissing like a camel as the Krug poured out of me. I thought about Priscilla and what I wanted to do to her.

I finished, approached the sink and began washing my hands. He hovered over me, his silly pink jacket invading my space. He passed me a hand towel, which I didn't thank him for, and then pointed to the selection of fragrances lining a shelf below the mirror and above the basin. The multicoloured bottles shone under the light, all different shapes and sizes. I said, 'No, thanks,' turned my back and made my way to the exit.

'You fucking what?' I turned around and faced him again. He said nothing and just smiled at me. I drew closer. 'What did you just fucking say?'

He continued to say nothing, and carried on smiling.

I stepped closer, a yard away. 'You called me a cunt, didn't you? Just as I turned around, under your breath you called me a cunt, because I never paid you.'

He didn't say anything, just stared back at me, his expression now blank.

'You think you've got a God-given right to stand there and get paid for handing me a towel you don't own and offering me a fucking spray from your shit collection of cologne.'

He still didn't say anything.

'Well, fucking do you?'

He definitely said it. I heard him for sure. Didn't I? Did I? He smiled again, as though nothing I'd said had gone in, and picked up a bottle from the shelf – a mauve colour, an oval shape. He offered me the bottle, still with that smile.

'Has nothing I said gone into that thick skull of yours?' I smashed my index finger into the side of my temple. 'This is not over!'

I turned away and made my way towards the exit, crashing through the door and exploding back out into

117

the restaurant like a madman. I felt the veins in my neck protruding. I was perspiring heavily from my forehead.

What the hell had come over me? Here we go again – that fucking pressure-cooker dial. I was losing the fucking plot. Why did I get so angry and irritated over a guy who just wanted to hand me a paper towel? Get out of the restaurant and enjoy the rest of your evening. Don't go back in there. You don't know what you could be capable of. What would you do? Rough him up? Or kill him, like her before?

Maybe I didn't give a shit now. Killed one, why not kill another? Maybe I wanted to get caught. Stop running. But I didn't want to get caught, I was sure of that. It was like killing Zenith Provoski had given me an appetite for it, a new powerful drug I hadn't yet explored until last night which gave me a buzz better than any line of coke ever did. Maybe that's why serial killers never stopped, they were always looking for their next hit. Was I a serial killer? Was I? After just one kill I guess I wasn't, but that could be arranged. I felt a tingle go through my body, a rush of excitement and adrenaline. Nothing else mattered right now.

The restaurant was now nearly empty. Just a young couple remained, early twenties maybe, very much in love. Their hands were locked across the table, their eyes fixed on each other. Tourists, I thought. I checked my watch. Priscilla would definitely have finished her smoke by now. Maybe she'd light another.

I drifted by the young couple's table. The girl was very attractive. Long blonde hair and stunning big blue eyes, she was wearing a strapless white dress that hugged her slender frame.

The guy then unexpectedly called me over, oblivious to my rage.

'Excuse me, sir, I'm so sorry to interrupt, but could you possibly take our picture? If it's not too much trouble, that is?'

Definitely tourists. Americans, not New Yorkers, but for sure the unmistakable and instantly recognisable twang of an LA accent.

I stared at her and she gave me a gorgeous smile. She was beautiful. I looked at him. He was a guy. In my head I was telling him to fuck off. I didn't have time for this shit. Priscilla would definitely be wondering where I was by now. Maybe she'd come back into the restaurant to look for me. I could have been rude, told him I was in a rush, but I didn't. I didn't because on their table I noticed something. It would be perfect.

'Sure,' I said. 'Not a problem.'

I took his phone. She shuffled in and put her arm around him, they smiled and I clicked away.

'One more?' I asked.

'Great,' he said.

I did the usual when taking someone's picture. I glanced at it and said, 'That's lovely.' Then I handed him the phone and waited for my chance. As they both looked at the photo and obsessed for a millisecond at the couple smiling back at them, I reached down, took his steak knife from the table and slipped it into my jacket pocket.

'Thank you,' they both said, looking back up towards me, unaware for now of my actions.

'Not a problem. Not a problem at all. Enjoy your meal.' And with that I headed back towards the toilets, quick, eager, an agenda to stick to. On the way I picked up a tablecloth from a stack piled in a station area. No one saw me.

As I entered the men's room he paid no immediate attention to me, just played around with his bottles of aftershave, rearranging them over and over again.

I stepped up behind him. He laughed at me in the reflection. I could have done it there and then – pulled the knife out of my pocket and stabbed him in the back – but it would have been easy. Far too easy. I wanted to see the pain in his eyes. I took a deep breath, inhaling his odour deep into my lungs. He smelled sweet, like candy, like a child. I was a few feet away from him, maybe less.

He turned and faced me, still laughing, pointing at

the tablecloth that was now wrapped around me. He rolled a fresh lollipop around his mouth. I could smell it in his saliva. Cherry. The sound irritated me. He waited, but not anxiously, as though my reappearance so soon hadn't fazed him.

I stared deep into his eyes. They were grey and lifeless, like a doll's. Not a drop of emotion. He continued to stare back at me, a blank, gormless expression, the stick of the lolly hanging out of the side of his mouth, like an unlit cigarette waiting to be sparked. Was this guy actually mocking me? Was he?

'Fucking say something, will you?' I snarled, my teeth bared.

He didn't. Instead, he turned away from me, picked up the same aftershave as before and offered it to me again.

I laughed. He laughed. We then laughed together. Then I pulled the knife from my pocket and stuck it straight through his neck.

Outside, it was cold. The sun had well and truly set and nightfall had slowly invaded Paris.

Priscilla was leaning against the car, wrapped in a thick shawl, smoking a cigarette that was definitely not her first.

I took one of my own from my pack and asked for the matches I'd lent her, then sparked up and stood next to her.

'What took you so long?' she asked. 'I was about to send a search party.'

'Sorry, got caught up chatting to some young couple. They asked me to take their picture.'

'I see you ran into Alberto,' she said.

'Sorry?'

Your aftershave smells different. Alberto is the washroom attendant. He's Léon's younger brother. He got him the job here so he can keep an eye on him.'

I had sprayed myself with some of his cologne, just after slicing his throat.

'Léon?' I questioned.

'Yes, Léon. The maître d' from the restaurant.'

'Sorry, Léon, yes. His brother is a nice guy. Had a nice chat with him.'

'A nice chat?'

Her tone changed instantly, the softness in her voice replaced with angry sarcasm. Her facial expression changed also. Lines appeared across her forehead, deep dark grooves that aged her ten years instantly.

'Yeah, a nice chat,' I said, bewildered.

'Alberto has had learning difficulties all his life.' Her voice was uptight and laced with emotion. 'He's also deaf and dumb.'

15

We'd decided to bypass the members only bar when she started caressing my penis in the back of the ride. I'd got round the whole Alberto incident by saying it was a joke that I'd spoken with him. A sick joke, she'd said, but managed to raise a smile after six blocks and then was stroking my groin by the seventh. They were obviously not that close.

Our destination was the Royal, her room, Pass Go, Collect £200. En route I asked about the stretch, a Mercedes-Maybach.

'Never had a ride in one of these,' I said.

'My brother demands them everywhere we go – won't settle for anything else.'

Money talks, I thought. 'Nice,' I said. 'Suppose it makes sense having chauffeurs who know the ins and outs of every city you visit.'

'Oh, no, Sebastian is mine. He comes everywhere with me – chauffeur stroke bodyguard.'

She went on to explain a bit about him. I was half-listening, as her hand had progressed way beyond my briefs. I was hard. I wanted more. A lot more.

Sebastian who?

We were back at the hotel after twenty minutes, a slight jam on the Avenue des Champs-Élysées delaying our arrival and my inevitable ejaculation.

As we got out of the car Sebastian told Priscilla he was going to grab a bite to eat outside of town. He'd heard about this steak-house that did the most amazing T-bones, the size of small cars.

'No problem. Enjoy,' Priscilla said, waving him off.

'Remember, it's half hour away,' Sebastian said. 'So if you need me, bear that in mind.'

'Not a problem. Now go and eat your small car!'

He smiled, wound the window up and slowly pulled away. For the next thirty minutes I was sure he would be dreaming of that T-bone.

We disappeared into the enchanting glow of the Royal, leaving Sebastian, the cordial welcome of the doorman and the wide smiles from the reception all behind us. We got into the lift. We kissed for the first time.

Priscilla had the penthouse suite. Of course she did. We drank champagne on the chaise-longue that sat in the bay window overlooking Paris and its outer regions. The conversation never really got going. We'd done all our talking that afternoon. We were both here for one reason only.

Within ten minutes Priscilla excused herself, telling me she was 'going to slip into something a little more comfortable.' I hoped by comfort she didn't mean her gym sweats.

While she was gone I thought about Alberto. Surely he would have been found by now? When I left the restaurant there was only one table remaining – the young couple. Maybe he'd found him. I checked my watch. 5:45 pm, that time between lunch and an early dinner. A change in shifts, day staff replaced by night. The young couple surely must have left by now. I'd taken the steak knife from a plate stained in blood, which meant his medium rare had been devoured and only dessert was left to follow. If my guy didn't need a leak before he left I had a slight window. I assumed the first covers for evening started at, say, 6:30. I maybe had half an hour to forty-five minutes before anyone entered the toilets again. But then there was Léon. Surely he would check on his brother at some stage. Yes, of course he would. The big brother looking out for his dumb-arse sibling. Fuck.

I hadn't thought this through. Killing Alberto was a big mistake. Huge. What was I thinking? How in God's name did I think I would ever get away with this? But I couldn't help myself. The temptation had been excruciating.

I had the taste for killing. It was like heroin – once was never going to be enough, twice was only going to whet my appetite.

I imagined what Léon might find – Alberto lying in a thick pool of fresh blood, a gaping hole in the side of his neck. I'd got him real good. I must have hit an artery, since the blood had pissed out of him like water from a hose pipe. It had been everywhere – the mirrors, the basins, me. Luckily I'd wrapped the tablecloth around me. It had done the job, and hardly a speck of blood had tarnished my clothes. My hands, however, had been covered. I'd spent five minutes scrubbing the absolute fucking hell out of the them with soap from the dispenser and a stack of hand towels. It had gotten deep into my fingernails. I'd needed a steaming hot shower and a scrubbing brush; neither was an option in the gents of the Jules Verne. I'd done the best I could.

Priscilla returned after five minutes in nothing but black high heels and black stockings. Her body was fucking amazing for a fifty-something. A toned stomach, great legs and even better arse – she must have worked out religiously. Her breasts were perky, a decent size. She'd definitely had work done; they were set high up her chest and were perfectly round.

It wasn't long before my trousers were off and she

was sitting on my dick, slow delicate movements driven at first from her hips. We explored each other's bodies using fine strokes and inquisitive fingertips. We kissed softly in between dirty whispers. The sex slowly became harder, exquisite touches replaced with forceful and unyielding clasps. The kissing became open mouths and deep tongues. No time for playful words now. She smelled fucking great; she tasted even better as I dived into her neck. She groaned at every bite, getting faster, wetter. I was deep inside her and she loved it.

Then all of a sudden the room telephone rang, an irritating *bzzt* that bounced off the walls. Who had the fucking nerve?

I told her to ignore it. She agreed. 'Probably my brother checking up on me,' she said.

The phone rang out and we continued, same pace, really going at it, no one else in the world but us.

'You've got to be fucking kidding me,' I said, as the phone started ringing again.

'I better check. It might be important.'

I rolled my eyes.

She got off my dick and whispered in my ear, 'Don't worry, we have all night.'

She moved across the room to the phone. I sat exposed, my dick erect – rock solid. I checked my fingernails meticulously in the shadowy light of the penthouse while waiting on the identity of the unexpected caller. I could still see traces of Alberto's blood.

Straightaway I knew there was something wrong. From the moment she held the receiver to her ear her face dropped and tears began to well.

The conversation was very one-sided. She must have said two words. When she eventually put the receiver back on its cradle, she kept her distance, speaking to me from across the room.

'Alberto has been murdered,' she said. Her voice was broken, the words muffled, as though I could have heard it wrong.

'What?' That was all I had at this stage.

'Murdered, tonight. Stabbed in the throat.'

'That's fucking terrible.' My palms were beginning to moisten, my rock-solid dick now lopsided and shrinking all the time. I got up and put my pants and trousers on, and started to walk across the room towards her.

'Stay where you fucking are,' she said.

'Baby?'

'You were in there. You must have been the last person in there. I'm sure the restaurant was empty apart from us.'

'You seriously don't think it was me, baby?'

'Stop calling me fucking baby. Six hours ago I didn't know you from Adam.'

You still don't, honey, I thought.

She was getting cranky. I desperately needed to defuse the situation. I stopped in the middle of the room, feeling a chill across my shoulder-blades from the air-conditioning unit above me.

'Listen,' I said. 'I left Alberto alive and well. Jesus, you really think I could be capable of doing something like that, after the afternoon we'd just enjoyed? Who was on the phone?'

'Léon.'

'How did he get this number?'

'He always knows I stay at the Royal.'

'What else did he say?'

'He wanted to know how long I was in town.'

'Why?'

'He said the police were asking for a list of everyone in the restaurant tonight. He told them he knew where I was staying. I wouldn't be surprised if they were making their way here right now.'

Fuck. 'Why are they coming here? Surely they don't think you, me, had anything to do with it?'

'It's an urgent murder case. They're going to want to speak with everyone. Get statements.'

'Were the police with him just now, when he called?'

'I don't know. He just said he had to tell them I was there this afternoon and had to tell them where I was

129

staying.'

'So why did he call you? Why didn't he leave it to the police?'

'He's a friend. That's what friends do.'

'I thought he was just a waiter at a restaurant you visited frequently?'

'Don't question my relationship with anyone. You don't know me. Six hours ago I was a stranger to you.'

She knew me well enough to let me stick my cock in her, I thought. Fucking whore. I bet there were a thousand of me. One-night stands spread across the globe.

'Anything else?' I asked, keeping it amiable for now.

'He wanted your background.'

'My background? What did you tell him?'

'Look, you fucking heard the conversation, right? I hardly spoke. He could hear I was in shock, so he said he'd call back later.'

'Sorry. Terrible business, all this. Look, I know we've only just met, but after today, surely you know I'm not capable of something like that?'

She paused, looked right through me, then stepped out of the room, returning in a dressing gown. Snug. No longer sexy. Compliments of the hotel.

'Did you see anyone else lurking about?' She was slightly more at ease now.

'Fuck, there was a guy,' I said.

'A guy?'

'Yeah, young guy, with a girl.' I thought about him, his face still fresh in my mind, Mr Polite-and-Handsome.

'A young guy, with a girl?'

'Yes, they were the only table left. Remember when I told you I took their picture? Maybe he used the toilet after me?'

She picked up her phone and started to punch numbers.

'Who are you calling?'

'The police. You can give a description of him. Maybe Léon remembered him also.'

'Listen,' I said, trying to calm her down. 'Let's both get changed, jump in the car and go to the police station. That way I can give a full statement on this guy.'

She stared at me for a second, the receiver to her ear, unsure. The room was ill-lit, the only source of light coming from the lamp next to her, its warm glow casting her shadow along the wall and up onto the ceiling.

'Come on, put the phone down. Let's leave right now.'

She took the phone away from her ear and cancelled the call. Thank fuck for that. It bought me some time, but not much.

'Maybe it would be quicker to go down to the station,' she conceded.

'The police station is only two blocks away. I passed

it yesterday. We'll be there in no time.' I wasn't lying. I'd seen it yesterday. I had no intention of seeing it again. 'I need a cigarette first, calm my nerves.'

'Of course, take your time. Terrible business all this. Just terrible.'

She seemed more at ease. Her knee-jerk reaction had mellowed, the thought of me being a killer defused by my convincing display of innocence.

She went over to the coffee table and picked up a box of smokes, a French label I didn't recognise. Long slim fags, the tobacco wrapped in a brown paper.

'Your matches?' she asked.

'My jacket pocket,' I said. 'Hanging on the door in the bathroom.'

She disappeared from the room and I was alone with my thoughts for a few seconds. A grandfather clock ticked in the background, the only sound.

I added a shirt to my trousers and looked for my shoes, which were next to the chaise-longue. I sat down with my back to the bathroom and continued to get dressed. The door creaked and the light from the bathroom entered the room. I could smell the smoke from her burning tobacco. With my back to her still, I said, 'I'll just run back to my room. I need some smokes of my own, then we can get your guy to take us to the police station.'

Obviously I had no intention of coming back. I would

get my money and get the fuck out of town. I got my shoes on, got up and turned round. She was standing by the toilet door, out of the light and in the darkness. All I could see was her vague outline and the orange glow of her burning cigarette.

'I'm pretty sure these rooms can detect smoke,' I said. 'But then again, I suppose they pretty much let you do what you like.'

She didn't reply, just kept still in the dark by the bathroom door, her only movement to take a drag. She was about forty feet away, possibly more. After all, this was a huge fucking suite in the Royal.

'Babe, step into the light so I can see you,' I said. She began to walk towards me. I found my cardigan and put it on. As I did up the buttons, I said, 'That's it, babe. There's nothing to be afraid of. I'm one of the good guys.'

The smell of her cigarette became more apparent as she edged closer, her footsteps agile on the soft, dense carpet beneath our feet.

Twenty feet away now. I gradually made out her features, not just an outline of a figure in the shadows. A cloud of smoke drifted into the light, hanging within the crimson glow of the red silk lampshade, like hell on earth. She came out of the darkness and stood where she'd been before, next to the phone, the cigarette in one hand smouldering away, her other hand in her dressing gown pocket. A tail of ash dropped on the floor. She didn't notice, her eyes were fixed on me, but distant, looking through me.

'You look dreadful,' I said. 'Terribly shocking, all this. Can I bum a smoke?'

She pointed to the coffee table, where her cigarettes were. 'Help yourself.'

I took one out of the box, the brand I didn't recognise, long and slim, wrapped in brown paper.

'Matches?'

She put what was now just a dying butt in her mouth and reached into her dressing-gown pocket, then chucked the matches towards me.

I sparked up, threw the matches on the coffee table and inhaled deeply. Menthol.

She glanced down at the matches on the table as I had my second drag, a bigger pull this time.

'I could not find them at first,' she said.

'Find what?'

'Your matches. I went to check your jacket. It has two inside pockets, you know. Well, obviously you do. It's your jacket, right? I guess most sports jackets of that style have two.'

I made to say something but she didn't give me a chance. She flicked her fag butt onto the carpet. Unusual behaviour, even in the circumstances. I took another drag and continued to listen.

'Dogtooth. I like dogtooth. I have a vintage Chanel dress in the same pattern.'

I focused down at the floor, where her dying butt gave off its last bit of smoke, like a deserted camp fire.

'Let me pour you a drink before we go,' I said. 'Do you have any brandy? Settle the nerves?'

'Over there.' She pointed to a drinks cabinet behind me, her other hand still behind her back.

I found a decent bottle of Rémy Martin and two crystal brandy glasses and poured a couple of large ones with an unsteady hand, splashing the mahogany surface with a good glug of decent liquor. After several attempts I screwed the cap back on the bottle then turned and made my way back across the room. She was standing in the same position, same pose, same distant expression. I got within ten feet of her, past the coffee table and the extinguished cigarette, and heard a phone ping and vibrate. Obviously it wasn't mine, as mine was accumulating unread text messages from a St Pancras waste-bin. I could not see it, so I guessed her phone was in her robe pocket. Maybe her brother checking in? Maybe Léon with an update? Maybe he was on to me? A discreet text to keep me where I was before the police turned up?

I reached out to pass her the drink, five feet away

maybe. She stopped me in my tracks, raising her hand.

'Stay the fuck there.'

I danced to her tune. She was fucking cranky. I took a sip of my drink. The strength took me by surprise, and I stuttered out my next words over a burning throat.

'Babe, you're in shock. I'm here to help.' Although I definitely was not.

'Two pockets. Your jacket has two pockets.'

Christ, here we go again, I thought, but I humoured her. 'Yes, most sports jackets do. Look, take your drink and calm down. This is obviously very traumatic for you, but don't be scared of me. I'm one of the good guys, remember? One of the good guys.'

'You see, I found your matches, but I checked the wrong pocket at first. Not intentionally. I wasn't snooping.'

'It's fine.' Jesus, where the fuck was she going with this? I put her rambling down to the shock. It wasn't every day you found out someone you knew had been murdered. I tried to offer her the drink again, a good nip would hopefully settle her, but she stepped back as I approached.

'Is it fine, though?' she said, her voice breaking with emotion.

I was starting to lose my patience. I should have been the hell out of there by now – a different hotel, a different lobby. A different girl on reception, not as pretty as Azurine.

'I'm going to go,' I said. 'I'll go to the police station and let them know everything. Hopefully they will nail the bastard. I'm sorry such a wonderful day has been tarnished by this.'

I knocked back the remainder of my drink, more prepared this time for the potent aftertaste.

'You're going fucking nowhere.'

'You fucking what?' Pressure cooker. The dial was being turned again. I could physically feel the blood rushing to my head, the veins on my temples erupting through my skin, my rapid heartbeat, the beads of sweat dripping down my face. I edged closer to her. I just wanted to get past her and to the door. It would be in her best interest not to try and stop me.

'I said stay where you fucking are.' She raised her voice immensely.

'I've tried to be reasonable with you, Priscilla, but don't fucking push me. I'm leaving this room now and there's nothing you can do to stop me.'

'Oh, yeah?' she said, confidently. 'Maybe this will change your mind, you sick bastard.'

She pulled her hand out of the dressing gown pocket and there it was, in all its fucking glory, the steak knife caked in Alberto's dried blood.

16

I'd been complacent with the knife. I should have dumped
it straightaway, instead of leaving it in my jacket pocket
like a fool. Fuck! I stood, I waited, I listened.

I remembered a place in my head, a small room
with blinding white walls, a window with a view of a
courtyard. I recognised it but couldn't place it. It was
better than here.

'I've texted Sebastian,' she said, breaking my train of
thought. 'He'll be here in minutes. He knows everything
and has also called the police.'

So that was who the incoming text message was from.
Sebastian. She must have messaged from the bathroom,
filling him in. I remembered some of what Pricilla had
told me briefly in the back of car. He was ex-army,
fucking SAS, mid- to late-fifties but still all muscle. He
was over six feet tall and had hands like concrete slabs.
It appeared like my run was well and truly over. Oh well,
it was good while it lasted.

I laughed at my predicament as she held the knife out in front of her. She was a bag of nerves, trembling.

I finished her drink and placed the glass down on the coffee table, savouring the taste in my mouth. My last ever?

'What now?' I said.

'We wait.'

I sat down on the coffee table, took another of her smokes from the packet, sparked up and settled in to it. My calmness put her on edge. I could see it in her eyes. She stood holding the knife out in front of her and kept glancing towards the door, a quick check, then eyes back on me.

Her phone rang suddenly, startling both of us. She stared at me and then down at the pocket of her dressing gown.

'Answer it, then,' I said, through a breath of smoke.

She took the phone out of her pocket, still holding the knife in front of her, the blade quivering.

'Sebastian.' Her voice was weak, broken. He must have been worried that she never responded to his message. The conversation was very one-sided, like when she'd spoken to Léon. After just a few seconds, the phone was back in her pocket.

'Well?' I said, stumping my butt into the glass ashtray alongside me.

'Sebastian is in the reception. So are the police. The hotel is fucking surrounded.'

'Well, I guess this is it, then. Don't mind if I pour myself one more drink as a condemned man, do you?'

I got up from the coffee table and picked up my glass.

'Stay where you fucking are.'

'Come on, babes. As you said, the hotel is fucking surrounded. Do you really think I'd be daft enough to try anything? I'm just going to walk over there and pour myself one last drink.'

I pointed to the drinks cabinet on the other side of the room, away from her. She nodded. I moved across the room, my back to her, and could feel her eyes burning through me.

'Why did you do it?'

I poured my drink, my back still to her. The Rémy Martin glugged through the neck of the bottle, a large one. I took in a mouthful and winced, then turned and faced her.

'I don't know. I really don't know. There's something wrong with me. I'm sick. I need help.'

'You're a fucking psycho, that's what you are.'

She glanced back towards the door – the police, Sebastian, any-fucking-one to get her out of here.

I made to reply but stopped. Sebastian. I remembered something he said in the car before we left: 'Remember, it's half hour away, so if you need me, bear that in mind.'

There was no way Sebastian was at the hotel. Not yet, anyway. I thought back to when she'd texted him, in the bathroom, when she discovered the knife. Only five minutes ago. We'd been back at the hotel for over an hour. He would have been at the bistro for sure when he received the text, up to his eyes in T-bone. He would have left straightaway, but that would mean he was still some way away, twenty minutes at a push. He would have called the police, and they would be on their way also. That was the phone call, advising Priscilla to sit tight. *'Tell him we're downstairs to stop him doing anything rash.'*

She was pinning her hopes on the police arriving first, and they would. And it would be very soon. A suspected murderer holed up with his next potential victim wasn't going to be taken lightly. But I had a chance. Not much of a chance but better than before – better than when I thought the hotel was surrounded already.

'Let me pour me you a drink.'

'I don't want a drink.'

I ignored her. I splashed Rémy Martin across two glasses this time and walked towards her.

'Stay where you fucking are.'

I carried on walking.

'I said stay where you fucking—'

141

I carried on walking, both glasses held out in front of me.

'Seriously one more step and I will—'

She waved the knife out in front of her frantically, her slim wrists riding out of her robe, her veins popping through the skin.

'Will what?' I said.

'I will kill you like you killed Alberto.'

I laughed. A loud sarcastic cackle. 'My dear Priscilla, come on. You could hardly carve a joint of meat with that knife, let alone kill someone with it. Look, I'm not going to try anything. As you say, the hotel is surrounded, and any second now an army of police will be bursting through that door and pinning me to the floor. Take the drink. You seriously look like you need it…'

I was now within arm's length of her. I held out the glass. She hesitated. The blade of the knife was inches from my face, so close I caught my reflection in it.

'Take it. Come on, it will do you good, I promise.'

She stared at me, transfixed, fear tarnishing her face. Her mascara was smudged and her cheeks sunken. It was as though the past ten minutes had added twenty years to her life, and she was a shadow of the woman who'd beamed in the restaurant.

My mind drifted for a split second – that place again, the small room, blinding white walls. A window looking onto a courtyard. There was a single bed, a small TV fixed to the wall by a swivel bracket. I had definitely been there, for sure. Hadn't I? There was a smell associated with it. Disinfectant. A strong smell of disinfectant. I could almost taste it.

She broke my train of thought for the second time as she slowly raised her left hand to take the drink. This was it. Now or never. I grabbed her arm and put it up against her back. She bellowed in pain, dropping the knife in her other hand in the process. I dragged her across the room. It was easy. She must only have weighed eight stone, at the most. *Bones dusted in flesh.*

I opened the doors to the balcony and shoved her outside, then locked the door. I had no intention of killing her. Alberto had already shown me that blood from a knife wound was horrific, and I couldn't walk through a hotel saturated in Priscilla's claret if I were to have any chance of escaping.

They would find her, sooner rather than later. I had a few minutes to try and get out while her screams were lost in the balcony of the penthouse suite.

I left the room and made my way to the fire exit in the corridor, and then down several flights of stairs to my floor. I found my room, I went in, I opened the safe. I shoved the money into one of the bags from Charlemagne's store.

I got out the room quickly, picking up a box of cigarettes and matches from the coffee table as I did so. The lift seemed to take forever. I was hot then cold, my mouth bone dry, my hands trembling. I finally reached the lobby. This was it. When the doors opened, I half-expected to be looking down the barrel of several guns, the Police Nationale all fucking over me. There was no one.

I walked past the reception and glanced over. The same two girls as before. I smiled.

'*Bonjour, monsieur*,' they said together.

I made my way to the front of the hotel, head down, and bumped into a chambermaid clutching a tower of folded towels. I apologised and side-stepped a UPS driver carrying a parcel to reception, tucked in his arm like a rugby ball. I kept going, in and out of people. I brushed arms with a lanky guy on his mobile phone. He glanced down and sneered at me. I ignored him, moved on. A party of middle-aged women were hanging around the revolving doors at the entrance, dressed up, ready to hit the town. I carved my way through them, politely, not making a scene. I breathed in their concoctions of rich scents, a melody of spices, flowers and oils. They smelled good, they looked good – particularly a tall, slim blonde, all legs and six-inch heels. We made eye contact. I said sorry for my intrusion. She stepped aside with a smile, and I passed her within a whisker, her long hair brushing my face as the cool night air fleetingly whirled around us. The revolving door spat out a porter grappling with two heavy suitcases. I got in after him, the chill hitting me hard as I made my way out to the steps of the hotel.

It certainly was cold. The breath spiralled from my mouth like a cloud of smoke from a cigarette. The doorman tilted his hat towards me. He was wearing black leather gloves that I envied. I nodded back with a thin smile, my eyes looking beyond him and out to the street.

I was expecting a sea of blue lights, a snake of white Citroëns roaring towards me, sirens echoing through the night. There was nothing.

I started to walk away from the hotel, east I think, heading towards the Champs-Élysées. I was on the main drag, city lights and bustling pavements, a wave of cars in both directions. I would be easy-pickings out here. Soon as the police had realised I'd escaped the hotel, they'd be scoping out the surrounding area. They would have a description of me from Sebastian, and Priscilla once she was found. I'd be all over their airwaves. I had to get off the street fast. I was surprised I'd even got this far. Why hadn't I been nicked in London? Why couldn't they trace me? There was CCTV everywhere these days, everyone of us living in our very own TV show.

It was a mystery. I was riding my luck, for sure, and at some point that luck had to run out, but I would keep going. Once this was over it would be over for ever, so I hailed a cab and got the fuck out of there.

I told the driver I wanted a hostel, somewhere cheap. I couldn't risk staying at another hotel and handing over my passport. The cheaper the hostel the better; I could pay cash with no questions asked. The driver spoke OK English. He said he knew of a hostel in Bondy, about ten kilometres outside Paris.

'Perfect,' I said, and got in the back.

We set off, back in the direction of the Royal, passing it. I slumped in my seat, peering across at the hotel as we ran alongside it. There was nothing unusual – the same doorman pacing the steps, no police, no sign of Sebastian's Mercedes.

We drove on, turning left at a T-junction and into a jam of red tail-lights.

'Fuck's sake,' I said, under my breath.

'Paris, it's like a giant car park,' said the driver. He wound down his window and sucked on an e-cigarette. I watched the cloud of smoke disappear into the night sky from my back seat.

'Is there another way?' I asked.

'This road leads you straight into Bondy, my friend. Don't worry, the road – how do you say in English?

Bottlenecks. Yes, bottlenecks about half a kilometre ahead. Once we're through that we'll be there in twenty minutes.'

'OK.'

I suppose I was relatively safe in here. What were they going to do? Search every car on the road? Maybe they would. Maybe they'd put blocks on all the roads leading out of Paris. Was I better off on foot? I thought for a moment about opening the door and getting the hell out, but where would I go? Paris would very soon be a hotbed of people looking for my arrest. I let go of the door handle, folded my arms and closed my eyes. Hopefully I would awake at my destination.

I don't know long it was – seconds, minutes, half an hour? I jumped upright, awoken by a cacophony of deafening sirens.

'What's going on?'

I was disoriented, half-asleep still, my eyes blurry. I looked ahead, the same fog of red tail-lights in front of us. Had we even moved?

'Big trouble, my friend. Big trouble.'

The taxi driver pointed towards his passenger window. When he opened it, I felt the cool night air wrap itself around my body. I was sitting in the centre seat in order to keep one eye on the traffic – well, keep an eye on it when I was awake. I shuffled across the worn leather of the aging Mercedes to the right-hand side of the car and wound down the electric window. More cold air, more noise. It had started.

A procession of police cars flashed by us, heading in the opposite direction, an acceleration of flashing blue lights moving as one. Then they were gone, their sirens echoing into the night behind us. I turned and watched them disappear through the smeared rear window. The hunt was now definitely on.

'Crazy,' said the driver, looking at me through his mirror. I just nodded back. He sensed my lack of enthusiasm to make conversation, and he was right. My head was spinning. He took the hint and turned up the radio.

I moved back to my seat. The traffic was still heavy up ahead. The car started to warm up again, and I slumped back, folding my arms and gradually closing my eyes. I didn't expect to fall asleep, but I did.

17

My eyes flickered into life and slowly adjusted to the light I must only have slept for an hour or so. I glanced up to see a damp ceiling and a single bulb hanging from a threadbare wire. The mattress beneath me cut through my spine. The bed-sheets smelled stale and were rough against my skin.

I slowly sat up and looked around. The room was small and dingy, nothing but a wash basin and cracked window for company. There were no curtains or blinds. Broad daylight bled through the room, revealing the squalor around me.

I got up. My body ached. The carpet beneath my bare feet was worn and stained. I dreaded to think with what. I made my way to the window. It was an old-fashioned sash window, and the wood around the frames was peeling away. I opened it right up and sat on the ledge. It was cold. January all around me.

I sparked up a smoke and took it right down. The buzz

of that first drag of the day filled me with a temporary satisfaction. It didn't last, it never does, but this morning it faded away quicker than ever before as I thought back to last night – my predicament, my comeuppance.

They knew who they were looking for now. I was a fugitive. My face would be splashed across TV screens and newspapers across the whole of Paris.

I stubbed my cigarette out on the window sill and stepped back into the room. Above the basin was a small rectangle mirror. I stared at my reflection. Yesterday's man, drab and weary. I splashed some cold water on my face and dabbed it down with a towel that was as coarse as sandpaper.

I was in the same clothes. They were crumpled but OK. I dusted myself down and straightened my collar then walked back to the bed. The bag of cash was still under the pillow. No thief in the night. I was a fugitive with means. I thought about what I was going to do next. I'd checked into the hostel for two nights. I didn't want to stay in any one place too long. I needed to travel as far away from Paris as possible, possibly making my way down to the south coast, the Riviera, and go out in style. But my thinking was foggy. I immediately remembered the hotels requesting identification, which was the main reason I was in this current slime hole. I had a bag full of fucking money and I couldn't even spend it. So what was I going to do? I would rather get caught than spend the remains of my freedom ducking in and out of flea-pit hostels.

I rolled my sleeve back and checked the time. 10:35. I was ravenous. I hadn't eaten since the Jules Verne yesterday afternoon.

I went back over to the window and peered out. Bondy. I was on the sixth floor. The suburb before me seemed run-down and drab, helped by its deficient society, no doubt. Dull grey high-rises were scattered across the skyline. It was ugly and colourless, a concrete ghetto hiding within the shadows of Paris.

I stepped back into the room and took it in. This was going to be it going forward, a life living in squalor. One bad neighbourhood would follow the next, one dilapidated room would merge into another. I would rather go to prison, I really would. So I made up my mind. I would take risks, pour everything into one day of decadence rather than a lifetime of austerity.

It was time to go back into the lion's den.

18

I'd taken a tram to the Avenue des Champs-Élysées, the hub of Paris. I strolled without any real purpose but with enough enthusiasm to find a restaurant. A good one. The whole place was buzzing. The district looked great under sunlight – lofty white buildings shadowing the avenue either side as far as the eye could see, sparkling under a winter sun that sat at its highest elevation, in a sky so blue it felt like it had been painted by Monet himself. The pavements were lined with elm trees cut into perfect rectangles. They dotted either side of the street and stretched through the whole avenue, shadowing the boutiques leading up to the famous Arc de Triomphe standing proudly on the horizon.

I danced in and out of tourists, led by a now diabolical yearning for food. Finally I stumbled across a cute-looking restaurant about halfway down the avenue. It had a large yellow-and-black striped canopy that stretched across the pavement, covering a dozen tables, maybe more, whose brilliant white tablecloths were held down by neat vases sprouting fresh flowers. The place was already heaving, which was obviously a good sign, but I managed to acquire a table for one, shown to me by a guy who was probably late fifties, or maybe early sixties. He was dressed differently to the other waiters, who were all wearing traditional white shirts and black trousers – or black skirts for the women, of whom I counted two. Both were young, slim and petite, and were dashing around waiting tables with a sleek, sexy elegance, doing a job they knew inside out.

My waiter wore smart navy chinos and a lime green shirt with a bright orange horse motif. I noticed his watch – a gold Rolex, the face covered in diamonds. He was either a waiter who'd had his hand in the till or, more likely, the proprietor of the establishment. He was bald, but the hair around the sides was long – shoulder-length, silver grey and wispy. He was clean-shaven apart from a thick, well-kept moustache that sat across his top lip like a fat, dormant slug. His eyes were piercing and an unusual shade of green, almost neon. He was slightly overweight, his midriff making the buttons on his shirt work overtime, but a good tan made him look healthy and prosperous. He would most definitely have been a good-looking man twenty years ago and was still mimicking certain aspects of his youth. He handed me two menus bound in a thick burgundy leather. Plonk and food. All I needed at this hour.

I scaled the wine list and chose a rather expensive Sauvignon. I also ordered a shot of absinthe. I was planning on getting fucked up; who knew how long it would be before they found me? I had to make every day as if it was my last.

My order delighted the proprietor. He seemed like the type that enjoyed a decent tipple and he kissed his fingers in appreciation of the chosen liquor. He went back to the restaurant, weaving in and out of tables with a slightly less panache than the waitresses, but then again, he didn't have to shake his arse for the tip jar.

I took out a smoke and eased back into my chair, leaving the menu closed on the table. I'd seen what I wanted chalked on the specials board on my way in.

The waitress approached with a wide smile. She was cute, early twenties, no more than five foot, with very short, bleach blonde hair. She had great dimples, and a small button nose and big blue eyes. She spoke with an accent but wasn't French. I hazarded a guess at Eastern European.

I ordered the squid from the specials but asked for skinny fries instead of rice. I was very specific in making sure they were in fact skinny fries and not regular chips – the type where you could get at least eight with one poke of a fork. She assured me they were what I was asking for. I took her word for it and handed her the menu back.

She disappeared through the maze of tables, passing the proprietor, who was advancing with my drink order.

'Holiday?' he asked, as he placed a tray on the edge of the table.

'Business,' I said, stubbing my cigarette out in a ceramic ashtray.

He unscrewed the cork from the bottle of wine with a captivating ease. 'Business good?' he asked.

'Not as good as yours,' I responded, glancing around the restaurant.

He laughed. 'Today is a good day.'

Indeed, I thought. It could well be my last.

He asked me if I wanted to sample the wine. I told him it was fine and to pour away. He did just that, then put the bottle into a stainless-steel bucket, that charming sound of ice shuffling as it nestled back into its place.

The winter sun was warm. I could have been sitting on the French Riviera. If I closed my eyes I could almost hear the waves slapping against the shore. I took a swig of wine and lit another smoke. The Sauvignon was perfectly chilled. It tasted great.

'Would you like me to prepare the absinthe, *monsieur*?'

I'd never drunk absinthe before. I'd just heard the

stories that it properly fucked you up. I'd assumed it was a neat liquor you drank as a shot – a sambuca, Jägermeister. You know, something along those lines. My ignorance was apparent, the pause in my reply revealing I was out of my depth.

'Sure,' I said, not fooling either of us.

He took a smallish glass and placed it on the table, then poured in a shot of the spirit, which was pale green in colour. He then placed a slotted spoon across the rim of the glass, on which he placed a small brick of sugar, before slowly pouring iced water from a jug onto the sugar cube and into the glass.

'The sugar quells the bitterness,' he said.

I nodded, transfixed, as it dissolved in the liquid. The colour of the spirit began to change, the clear emerald green transforming to a lighter, opalescent, milkier shade. I licked my lips.

'*Monsieur.*' He placed the glass out in front of me.

'*Santé.*' I raised it and took a drop. I was pleasantly surprised. It had a sweetness to it and not the pungent kick I was expecting.

'You are now in the hands of the green fairy, *monsieur.*'

'The green fairy?'

He pulled up the chair next to me and joined me at the table. 'The green fairy is an apparent figment of the drinker's imagination who would sit on their shoulders and guide them through a mystical journey.'

'Is that so?' I said, through a puff of smoke, my tone sneering.

'*Monsieur*, it is true. Two or three glasses of this,' he shook the bottle in front of me, 'and you will see things very differently.'

'In what way?'

He got up from the table and pushed the chair back into place. His smile was the kind of smile that had something behind it.

'You are in good company, *monsieur*. Oscar Wilde, Ernest Hemingway and Vincent van Gogh, to name but a few, were all avid drinkers of absinthe, and all of them succumbed to the dubious charms of the green fairy, who would enter their minds and tamper with their darkest inner thoughts.'

'So you're saying one is enough, then?' My tone was more serious than before.

'I'll leave you with this thought, *monsieur*. Oscar Wilde once said, "After the first glass of absinthe you see things as you wish they were. After the second you see them as they are not. Finally you see things as they really are, and that is the most horrible thing in the world.'

There was silence. We stared into each other's eyes for a brief second, just us, no one else in the world.

'Understood,' I said finally.

'Enjoy your meal, *monsieur*.' And he left the table, leaving me alone with my thoughts.

Two hours later I entered the slipstream of a slow-moving crowd, a school of tuna swimming towards the Arc de Triomphe. I was stuffed, I had eaten like a king. If that was going to be my last meal as a free man, I would succumb to being a condemned man, full to the brim.

I moved with a swagger. Well, in my mind, anyhow. To others it must have appeared more like the irritating zigzag of an intoxicated passerby. I was definitely now in the hands of the green fairy. Four glasses of the stuff had seen to that.

19

I stumbled across the Pink Chameleon at 5 pm. The bar was tucked away down a cobbled side-street in the heart of the Marais district, which I'd been told was the place for a drink. The entrance was quite small – more of a doorway really, under a neon sign in electric pink. The C and the first E in Chameleon had lost their illumination, while the N flickered, with an irritating buzzing sound that echoed through the narrow alley.

There was one doorman. He was huge, well over six foot tall and nearly as wide. He was a white guy with thick dreadlocks that twisted out from his scalp like the snakes from Medusa. His nose was pierced with a stud, his whole neck was inked with a thick spider's web that extended from his torso and stopped below his chin. I wondered if his whole body was a gigantic web.

'Coming in?' he said, his voice softer than I'd imagined.

I hesitated for a second. I could feel myself swaying

from side to side, the green fairy rocking at my shoulders.

'Sure, why not?' Like I needed another drink.

I'd left the restaurant about half an hour ago, stumbling around the city without any real purpose, leaving myself wide open.

'Straight down the stairs and pay Sam on your left.'

'OK, thanks.'

I definitely should have gone back. Leaving the money behind for so long was a risk. I'd managed to rip a floorboard up and store it underneath. The digs I was in didn't come with a safe – you were lucky to get a key for your door, a blind for the window, somewhere to piss.

Despite this moment of irresolution I went in, straight down the stairs, paying Sam on the left. Sam was a fit twenty-something blonde with huge tits busting out of a boob tube. It was a welcome surprise. I'd visualised Sam being a guy, something to do with an uncle I had of the same name. That's where the similarity ended. She wore a white mini skirt and black knee-high boots. She looked like she could go all night. I bet she did.

It cost me 10 Euros to get in. I paid from a roll of notes and got a stamp on my hand for my trouble. A set of double doors led to the club – the heavy type, smoke doors, no windows. I was closely followed by the green fairy.

20

Inside the club it was dark, the type of place where daytime never existed. There was a bar running down the right-hand side, and on the far wall a stage with a DJ booth behind it, which was unoccupied at this hour. Just a CD spinning on repeat, chill-out music. Down the left-hand side there were half a dozen booths for customers, dark red leather seats. They could probably hold six, maybe eight at a squeeze. Two were occupied, the other four empty, waiting for clientèle. The bar had ten stools, all taken apart from one. Some guys sat alone, others in conversation. The rest of the space consisted of a black-and-white chequered dance floor, which was scuffed and run down.

I moved over to the bar and sat at the one remaining stool, the last of the ten, nearest to the door. No one paid me any attention. The barman approached – an oldish guy, maybe sixty but trying desperately to look younger. He had long grey hair tied back in a ponytail, and his face was pumped with Botox. He had good teeth – white and probably bleached a thousand times. You could see he worked out, as his muscles were pumped against a short-sleeved fitted shirt that had been bought two sizes too small to emphasise the effect. His skin was dark and his eyes even darker. He smelled of weed. A hippy back in the day who still enjoyed the occasional joint. I had no problem with that.

'Hi, what will it be?'

'Bottle of beer please.'

'French?'

'Sure, why not? When in Rome and all that.'

'Or even Paris,' he said with a raised eyebrow. I laughed.

He leaned down to one of the several glass-door fridges in a row behind him, pulled out a dark green bottle and popped the cap on a bottle opener mounted to the inner side of the bar. He placed a coaster in front of me – not one of those good cardboard ones you could flick and catch off the side of a table but its flimsy relative. The beer was ice cold. You could tell by the condensation running down the outside of the bottle. It looked good. A marketing dream. Why, if I could take a picture of it right here and now and have it blown up on a giant billboard towering over some freeway, I'm sure it would get the most devoted teetotallers scrambling for the exit, looking for the nearest supermarket chain. Add a guy with a chiselled body and some tight swimming trunks and I reckon you could have got Demi Lovato off the wagon.

'Eight Euro, please,' he said.

I paid with a fifty from the same roll as before and waited for my change, taking a swig in the process. The beer tasted as cold as it appeared. The bartender returned with my 42 Euro, a mixture of notes and coins. I left it on the bar in front of me.

'When does it start getting busy?' I asked.

'Should pick up within a couple of hours, and then by eleven, twelve you won't be able to move for wall-to-wall cock.'

I nearly spat my beer all over him. 'What?'

'Come on, *monsieur*, the Pink Chameleon. Like you never knew.'

He gave me a wink and left me with my thoughts. I took another sip of beer. Not as good as the first, but then it never was. I looked around. Not a single *mademoiselle* in the house.

I thought about leaving. This definitely wasn't my scene. However I felt safe in here, away from prying eyes, prolonging my freedom. So instead, I ordered up another beer.

My drink arrived with a smile, the same white teeth

gleaming in the darkness. I paid and gave him a fifty on top.

'For you. Keep them coming.'

'Thank you, *monsieur*.'

'No problem. Just see I never have a dry glass.'

He put the note in the top pocket of his tight shirt and then attended two new guys who'd just walked in. One ordered a beer as the other flirted with the cocktail list before finally ordering a mojito. They were young guys, in their mid-twenties at a push, and very well-groomed. Neat beards and blow-dried hair, smart and spotless running trainers that had never seen a track, tight-fitting jeans and T-shirts displaying good physiques. I had them down as locals due to their deep conversion with the bartender. Regulars. A couple. Maybe they'd met here.

I checked my watch – 5:45 pm – and glanced towards the double doors, which were still and not swinging on their hinges. No one else yet. I visualised Sam on the other side, on the phone maybe, passing the time. I thought about her great breasts. I thought about her going all night, on top, hot and steamy, dirty. I imagined her legs wrapped round my head. I imagined her vagina, shaved, tight.

I turned back to face the room. The two well-groomed guys were now chatting to each other as the bartender stacked a shelf with fresh glasses from a dishwasher draped in a blanket of steam.

I thought of Sam again. Last chance saloon. Get up, walk out, flash her some cash, presuming she was that type of girl, and disappear into the evening arm-in-arm, forgetting this place ever existed. I sucked on my beer, took it all in.

Despite my wavering thoughts I didn't leave. Instead, I signalled to the bartender and he brought me another, ice-cold like the first, and the one after that.

I then sat and waited, a stranger in the background, a new guy in town.

21

At 11 pm, the bartender was right, the place was heaving.

I'd drunk myself sober, the green fairy now occupying someone else's shoulder. I sat on the same stool, in the background, near the double doors, a security blanket in case I wanted to get out fast.

I ordered a shot. I needed to get back in the game.

'Six Euros, please.'

'I'll get that.'

He came from nowhere, through the mist of bodies around me.

'*Bon soir*,' he said.

'Hi.'

'English?'

'Yes'

'Fucking great, my French is patchy to say the least. Sorry to intrude, but it seemed like you were on your own?'

The bar stool next to me had been free for about five

minutes. The previous occupant, a big guy, all skin with a love for martinis, was now strutting his stuff in the centre of the dance floor. He had no real rhythm, all arms and legs, high on life – maybe high on something else?

I stuttered for an answer, and eventually blurted out, 'Yes, I am.'

'Mind if I join you?'

Fuck, was this guy coming on to me? Of course he fucking was, I was sitting in a gay bar on my own. I might as well have been wearing a T-shirt that said free and single.

I hesitated. I couldn't think straight for the loud music, an insolent noise that rattled right through me.

My dithering was obvious, maybe he would lose interest and walk away, but he didn't, he just stood there waiting for his answer like the accused in front of a jury.

'Sure,' I finally said. I didn't know why. I just went with it. What the hell. If he came on to me I would just tell him I was straight, simple as that. Wasn't it?

He sat down. I glanced across the dance floor to where martini guy was still dancing, still no rhythm.

'Martin,' he said, putting out a hand.

I gave a false name.

He was about six foot tall, medium build. His hair was shaven, a number three all over, bleach blonde. He was wearing round, black-rimmed glasses. His eyes looked blue but it was hard to tell down here in the ill-lit basement.

He appeared to be in his early thirties, a good few years younger than me.

'Do you come here often?' I said. Cheap line, but it was all I had.

He laughed, showing a full set of veneers, dazzling white. 'Bet you say that to all the boys.'

I laughed too.

'Actually it's my first time here, the club and Paris – France, as a matter of fact.'

'What brings you here?' I asked.

'Work. I start a new job next Monday.'

'Oh, really? What line of work are you in?'

'Insurance. Frightfully boring. How about you?'

'Banking. Equally boring.'

We both laughed again.

'So how come Paris?' I went on.

'I hope you're sitting comfortably.'

I was. He had a lovely manner. The initial tension had dropped and I started to feel comfortable again.

'I have all night,' I said, downing my shot.

He had a beer. He took a sip. 'Well, you don't have to be Einstein to work out I'm gay. I didn't stumble across this place hoping to find naked women sliding up and down poles. I was hoping to hook up, and there you were.'

He smiled. I felt uneasy and it must have shown.

'Sorry, didn't mean to make you feel uncomfortable.'

'It's fine,' I said. Was it?

It then struck me that Martin was definitely hitting on me. This was not a passing conversation but could actually lead somewhere. The thought made me tense up a bit, dry mouth and a nervous fidget. I thought of Sam, last chance saloon, going all night.

Martin continued, 'So I am basically running away.'

'Running away from what?' I asked, showing real interest.

He took another sip of his beer, and I ordered two more. He offered to pay but I told him to put his money away.

'Feel like I'm going to get real deep here pretty soon. You sure you want to hear this?'

I wasn't sure, far from it. Part of me wanted to leave, get the hell out and return to my squalor. But I didn't. What did I have outside the doors of this club? I was a man on the run. Sooner or later they would catch up with me for sure. Down here I felt safe. Someone else. A different life – for now anyhow.

'I want to hear it,' I said, while at the same time my voice vibrated with uncertainty.

Martin dragged his stool into the bar, rested both arms

and nursed his beer between the palms of his hands, like a warm cup of coffee. 'My mother died when I was only young so I was brought up by my aunt.'

'What about your father?' I asked.

'He was ex-military, RAF, twenty years' service as a fighter pilot. He lost an arm when he was shot out of the sky over Iraq.'

'Fuck me.'

'At least let me buy you one more drink first.'

I felt myself blush, as if every drop of blood in my entire body had rushed straight to my head. I felt uneasy. Sick, in fact. What the hell was I doing here? The club, this situation, I was way out of my depth.

'Sorry, I didn't mean to embarrass you.'

Shit, was it that obvious? I should have made my excuses there and then, faked a call. Shit had just hit the fan at work, a dead relative... anything! For whatever reason, I didn't. Maybe it was the alcohol, maybe it was the inevitable waiting for me beyond the fire doors. They may have traced me here by CCTV. Maybe right now there was a wall of armed police waiting for me in outside the club.

I visualised my body sprawled below the pink neon lights, kissing the pavement, blood oozing from the side of my head from the gunshot wound.

Quick and easy.

'Are you OK?'

'Yeah fine, sorry,' I said, insincerely.

'I didn't mean to be crude.'

'You weren't, honestly. Please carry on.'

'I'm not going to bore you with the gory details. Christ, we're meant to be here for a bit of fun, right?'

I nodded, although I imagined his idea of fun was a completely different fucking ballpark compared to mine.

'At least give me the scaled-down version,' I said, more convincingly this time.

Martin took a swill of his beer, half a glass, ready to divulge. 'After Dad returned we moved back into the family home, just me and him, rattling around in a mock Tudor mansion. We had plenty of money. Dad had inherited a small fortune from his late father, a property tycoon.' Martin paused. 'I know, sounds terrible so far, doesn't it? Poor little rich kid.'

I didn't say anything, although it was what I was thinking.

'It really was terrible though, the worst time of my life.' Martin paused again and stared into space, clearly putting himself back there, reliving the moment. For a second the banging music faded away, no one else in the bar apart from us. 'Dad had been given honourable discharge,' he went on. 'A collection of medals. In everyone's eyes, including mine, he was a fucking hero,

171

but he just saw himself as a useless cripple. He suffered terribly with PTSD, and started drinking heavily. I was fifteen when he came back. Just before I was twenty he tried to kill himself.'

'Christ,' I said, choosing my reply more carefully this time.

'That's not the worst of it. On my twenty-first birthday, and after far too many drinks, I decided it was the right time to tell him I was gay.'

'Lead balloon?'

'Big fucking lead balloon. He chucked me out there and then.'

'What did you do?'

'I was lucky. I wasn't working at the time – in between jobs, finding out what I wanted to do, finding out who I really was. My mum had left me some money in a trust fund, enough to survive. For the next two years I bummed about in shitty rented accommodation in London, getting drunk and shagging about. I was a fucking mess. Then I met Ruby.'

'A girl?' I said, surprised.

'Nothing like that. A pure convenience thing. She had a room to let out, it was out of town, and I needed to get out of London. Every night I'd been out drinking and taking drugs, then back round to some stranger's house for another meaningless fuck. My life was going nowhere and I was digging myself into an early grave. Ruby was my saviour.'

'So how did you end up here? Paris?'

'Ruby was a Parisian. She'd moved to England when she met her husband and he had to relocate due to his job.'

'So you lived with them both back home?'

'No, I never met him. He'd died a few years back. Jumped in front of a train.'

'Fucking hell. Why?'

'Ruby said he suffered terribly with depression. Fucking tragic. She was a mess for years after but finally got her shit together and was planning to come back to Paris, even securing her old job.'

'So she is with you now?'

'She also died, a month ago today. Brain tumour. Before she died she persuaded her old company to take me on. She wanted me to make a fresh start, so here I am.'

'Christ, hell of a story. I'm sorry for your loss.'

'Thanks. It's been a rough ride, for sure. She was like a mother to me.'

There were a few seconds when neither of us said anything. The thumping bass of the music was more apparent now than before. It hurt my ears.

I was thinking what to say next, a way to lighten the

173

mood. I was just about to point out a guy on the dance floor who had taken off his T-shirt and wrapped it around his head when Martin's phone flashed up on the bar.

He picked it up and apologised for the intrusion.

'No problem.' I tried to get the barman's attention as Martin read a message. The phone lit up his face. His eyes were indeed blue. A very pale blue.

'Sorry about that. Email from my future employer.' He put his phone back on the bar.

'All OK?' I was still wating to grab the barman's attention with a folded fifty.

'Yeah, I was just meant to meet the owner of the company for lunch before I started. He can't make it now. Out of the country on business. Shame. I was looking forward to it. Right, I need to pee.'

Martin got up and left his phone, which was still alight. I watched him make his way towards the other side of the bar and picked it up. The email was still on the screen. I didn't know what I was looking for – a browse through his photos, text messages, who knew? I might not have been the only one playing a game here. I started reading the email.

Dear Martin,
I hope you're settling in to Paris life.
Sincere apologies but I won't be able to keep our

lunch appointment this week. Something has come up meaning I will be out of the country for a few days. I will be back in the office midday of your first day, so I will catch up with you then. It's a shame, as I was looking forward to seeing you in person before you started. I can only apologise again for the breakdown in technology on the Zoom interview. Usually I wouldn't hire someone off the back of a telephone interview, but due to Ruby's highly recommending you I am very confident you will fit in just perfectly. Keep up the French lessons. You'll get by for now, but in the long term will help you immensely.

Remember your passport on your first day for proof of identity. Until then enjoy the city and I will see you on the 27th.

Kind regards

Alfredo

I checked out the address line. Martin.Hawker80@ gmail.com. I put the phone down and locked it.

Martin made his way back through the crowd about two minutes later. I was still waiting to be served, my arrangement with the barman conveniently forgotten.

'Do you fancy going somewhere quieter?' I asked him.

'Sure. Where do you have in mind?'

'Somewhere we can hear ourselves think and maybe get served?'

Martin laughed.

'Sure. Let's get out of here.'

A minute later we were standing at the entrance of the club, my ears still ringing from the music. A wall of armed police was not waiting for me thankfully.

Outside the cool night air felt amazing against my skin, away from the sweatbox of the Pink Chameleon.

Martin was excited, like the night had only just begun. 'Right, where we headed?'

'Don't mind. Shall we—?'

His phone started ringing, interrupting me. He pulled it from his pocket and glanced at the display. 'My landlady. At this hour? Sorry, I should take this.'

'No problem.'

He turned away, stepping into the darkness. '*Oui*, Magdalene.'

Martin moved away from the club, taking shelter from the rain in a small bandstand in the centre of a pedestrianised street. It reminded me of the one in the courtyard. Where was that place? I'd been there for certain. Hadn't I?

I took out a cigarette and lit it, pulling hard on it, anticipating that first hit of nicotine and the rush that comes with it.

I coughed, I spluttered, I chucked it on the floor. The fucking fag reeked of bleach. What the hell?

'Sorry about that.'

I felt a hand touch my waist. It startled me as it had come from behind. I was now facing the club, watching a queue expand beyond the canopy.

'You OK there, jumpy?' Martin, a big grin on his face, both hands now on my waist as we faced each other. It made me uncomfortable.

'Yeah, sorry, wasn't expecting you to finish the call so soon. Everything OK?'

'Her mother is sick. She has to get out of town for a few days.'

'So you have a place here in Paris then?'

'A small rented flat. It's not much, but it's enough for me.'

'Sounds perfect.'

Suddenly I felt really envious of Martin, his fresh start and his perfect new life ahead of him. How I would kill to be in his shoes.

'So where are we headed?' he said exuberantly.

'Why don't we go back to yours?'

'Well, I've only been living there a couple of weeks and there are still boxes everywhere, but yes, that sounds great. If you're sure?'

I knew what Martin was getting at by asking if I was sure. He knew if I said yes I would be a dead cert. I went along with it.

'I'm sure.'

We hailed a taxi. The warmth and dryness of its back seat was more than appealing. Martin leaned forward, gave an address and then settled back. He put his arm around me, making me feel uncomfortable in the presence of a straight man. Well, a man I presumed was straight. I was on edge. I felt the driver's eyes burning down on me through his rearview mirror. Judging me, looking on with disgust, wishing he'd left us by the side of the road. Nevertheless, I kept up the pretence.

'How far is it?' I asked, burning up inside.

'Five minutes, that's all.'

For the rest of the journey I didn't say another word. I just closed my eyes. Five minutes felt like forever. I listened to the rain hitting the roof of the black Mercedes, I listened to the wipers rubbing against the windscreen. The wheels bumped over a cobbled street, the motion knocking my head against the window and causing me to open my eyes for a brief second. I peered out at the pouring rain and the passing street lamps, then a twenty-four-hour supermarket lit up like a Christmas tree on a corner. I closed my eyes again, the hot air from the AC sending me asleep like a toxic chemical.

I couldn't have been out for long but it felt like an eternity. I was drained. The day was now taking its toll. I reckon I could have slept for hours, days even, protected from reality in the repose of endless dreams.

I was woken by Martin gently shaking my shoulder. 'We are here.'

22

The lobby was narrow and rectangular in shape. The walls had a drab patterned wallpaper that had faded with time. The light was faint – two small lamps covered in worn velvet shades with fraying tassels, placed on a scratched mahogany sideboard, provided a warm but minimal glow.

There was only one elevator shaft, the metal door carved with graffiti. The carpet beneath our feet was threadbare and dirty, the ceiling above our heads low, the Artex peeling away in several places. The Royal it was not.

Martin pressed the button to the elevator. We heard the grinding of the metal cables above us as it descended.

'You OK?' Martin said.

'I'm fine. Just came over funny in the car. Too much to drink, that's all.'

The metal door opened in front of us, a sluggish slide that screeched a piercing, echoing cry in the night.

We stepped in. It smelled damp. Similar graffiti lined the inner walls – scratched initials and dates, lovers declaring their partners in the jagged lines of etched hearts.

Martin punched a number with his index finger. Four. There were only four floors, and I wasn't expecting a penthouse suite. We rose through the shaft, the same grinding sound of the metal cables distracting us from the awkward silence that had fallen.

The fourth floor was a small square shape, two doors to the left and two to the right, facing each other, no more than a dozen footsteps between them. The wall opposite us had the same drab wallpaper as the lobby, and a small rectangle-shaped window that probably never opened. Beneath the window was a small table supporting a lamp covered in the same worn velvet shade with fraying tassels. I imagined that the whole building was full of them, and once upon a time shiny and new. Martin stepped out of the lift and headed toward the door on the left. I followed. Silence, just the rain against the rectangle window.

Martin opened the door. He went in. I followed.

Apartment 7a was anything but a penthouse suite, just as I'd predicted. It was a small studio with minimum furniture, the kitchen mingling with the living room. There were only two doors off the main space, which I presumed were the bedroom and the bathroom. It wasn't much but it was neat and clean. Perfect for one person. Two would be company, three definitely a crowd. There were boxes everywhere, some unpacked, some half-unpacked and some not even open at all.

'Make yourself at home,' Martin said as he rattled around a cupboard, looking for some glasses.

I sat down on a two-seater sofa. The leather was hard and cold. There was a square glass coffee table with a book on it. *Fluent in Three Months*. I picked it up and started flicking through the pages.

'Vodka OK?' Martin called.

'Great,' I said.

In the background I could hear the glug of vodka as it escaped from the neck of a bottle.

'Ice?'

'Please.'

He joined me on the sofa – two were company – and passed me my drink.

'Thanks.'

He took a swig from his glass and then ran his hand over his buzz cut. It was like mine, just a different colour.

'So you don't speak French yet?' I said, pointing to the book.

'No. The book's a start, but I'll need to take lessons at some point.'

I thought back to the email, his employer recommending he should take lessons.

'So did you come to Paris for your interview?'

I knew full well he hadn't, but I had to be a hundred percent sure. He might have had a telephone interview and not yet met this Alfredo in person, but how was I to know he hadn't met a future colleague since then, arriving for an informal coffee or something? I needed to probe, get all the facts straight and clear in my head.

'No, I had a telephone interview a few weeks back which was just a formality. I spoke with the owner of the company. He was a good friend of Ruby's. I've only been here just under a week, hence the mess. Apart from you, I haven't met anyone yet.'

'I think the place looks great.'

I wasn't thinking about the apartment. That was the last thing on my mind.

'Thanks,' Martin said. 'I'll get there. '

'You said you haven't met anyone apart from me. You must have met your landlady, right?'

'Not even her. She left me a key in a safe box. I was meant to be meeting her tomorrow. That's why she called, told me she'd let me know when she was back in town.'

My head began to spin, and not from the alcohol.

Martin kept talking. His lips moved but no sound

came out. A small walnut of an idea that had been rattling around in my skull was now a swelling tumour the size of a fucking watermelon. Martin continued talking, smiling and gesturing, but I just looked straight through him, my brain doing overtime.

'I'm just going to freshen up,' I said, cutting him short in a sentence I didn't know the beginning of and now would never know the end.

'Fine.' There was a slight whimper to his voice, an unhappiness to my bluntness. 'Are you sure you're OK?'

I reassured him. 'I take it those two doors lead to the bedroom and the bathroom? You tell me which one is the bathroom and I'll see you in the bedroom shortly. Take the vodka and be ready for me.'

'Bathroom to the right,' he said with a smile, then disappeared through the other door, loosely clutching a bottle of Grey Goose.

I entered the bathroom and switched on the light by a cord. A small space – a bath, toilet and sink surrounded by fresh white tiles. Above the sink was a small mirrored wall cabinet. I leaned on the sink and stared at my dreary reflection, running the idea over and over in my head.

Could I really make it work? Could I?

I turned on the tap and splashed my face with cold water, then went back into the living room and towards the kitchen area. There was a set of car keys on the workspace, a chunky plastic car rental company's keyring attached. I opened up a drawer. Nothing but opened letters and an array of paperwork. One was an invoice from the car company. The rental was due back Monday.

His voice from the bedroom startled me. 'You OK?'

'Sorry, I felt a bit dehydrated. Just grabbing a glass of water.'

'There's Evian in the fridge.'

'Great. One second.' I shouted loudly, like he was in the next city instead of the bedroom, and opened up another drawer. Spoons, forks and knives all separated neatly in a plastic cutlery tray. I picked up one of the knives and ran my finger lightly across the jagged edge. It would have trouble cutting through hot butter.

'Hey – do I need to come and get you?'

I didn't know what to expect in the bedroom but I had an idea, and it turned my stomach.

'You won't be disappointed, I promise.'

I took off all my clothes apart from my briefs and scoped the kitchen one last time. Nothing. I started walking towards the bedroom, the tiled floor cold against my bare feet. The rain was tap-tapping at the window. I stopped outside the door. My heart was racing, I could feel every beat. I reached for the doorknob, my hand was shaking. The door clicked open. A warm glow of light filled the gap between the frame and the door. I could smell scented candles. I went in.

The room was a decent size. Square, windows on the right and a fitted wardrobe on the left. There were a few more boxes scattered about.

The back wall was natural brick, its orangey hue flickering in the candlelight.

The bed was in the centre of the room, the headboard flush against the brickwork. It looked like suede, expensive. Either side of it were matching cabinets, wood painted an off-white, made to look old. On top of each was a cast-iron candlestick-holder supporting long thin candles.

The bedsheets were a crisp white. On top of them lay Martin. He was naked and hard.

'What took you so long?' he whispered, grinning from ear to ear.

'Sorry, pre-match nerves, I guess. It's been a while.'

'Don't worry, I'll be gentle with you. Don't be shy.' He pointed to my briefs, then patted the side of the bed for me to join him. I felt sick. I could have vomited there and then. I didn't, though. I kept it together. I only had to keep it together for a couple more minutes. I knew what I was going to do as soon as I entered the room.

I took off my briefs and lay down next to him. He turned and looked me in the eyes.

'So who is fucking who?' he said.

I could smell the vodka on his breath, he was that close. Before I knew it he had his hand wrapped around my dick and his tongue in my mouth.

I pulled away.

'Turn over,' I said.

Martin smiled at me, a deep passionate smile that meant something, like he'd fallen for me hook, line and sinker. He turned over, no questions asked, burying his face in the pillows. It would be the last smile he'd ever give. I picked up one of the candlestick-holders and smashed it into the back of his head several times.

23

Fuck what had I done? How the hell was I going to get away with this? Twenty minutes had gone by and I was still standing over the bed in a daze, looking down at him.

There was fucking blood everywhere, the once dazzling white pillowcases and bed-sheets now oozing in a crimson tide. The headboard and surrounding brick wall were splattered with the liquid that once circulated around his body. The laceration to his head was wide open and raw. I could see part of his brain.

I finally snapped out of it. I didn't have much time if I was going to make this happen. I scoped out the kitchen again, looking for something different this time. Most of the cupboards were empty, just a scattering of odd glasses and plates.

The apartment was a sea of boxes. All shapes, all sizes. I didn't have time to start going through them all.

I then remembered the supermarket, lit up like a

Christmas tree. It wasn't far. We'd stopped shortly after passing it, and it was possibly on the same road.

I took a shower, hot to the point of scalding, and scrubbed hard at my skin with a nail-brush to remove the blood that covered my body. When I'd finished there were still traces beneath my fingernails. It would have to do for now. I got dressed, my clothes still damp from the rain, and picked up the car fob from the kitchen worktop.

I left apartment 7a at 1 am. I only had a few hours before dawn.

Outside the rain was still pouring heavily. Gutters spilled onto the streets, the sound of running water everywhere. I realised I didn't have a clue what he was driving. I checked the fob in my hand. Fiat. I headed down the road with the rain hard on my face. There were cars parked on both sides of the cobbled street, bumper to bumper, no more than a fag paper between them.

I came across a white Fiat, a small 500. I clicked the fob. Nothing. I kept going until I came across another. Same model but a darker colour.

I clicked the fob and the lights flashed.

Inside was small and basic, plastic everywhere. A bunch of little tree air-fresheners, in a rainbow of colours, hung from the rearview mirror. They smelled sweet and sickly. I adjusted the seat and stuck the keys in the ignition. It turned over after the third attempt, a slight hum and rattle.

I got on my way, in the direction I believed we'd come from, slow and easy, every cobble registering the deplorable suspension.

After two minutes, maybe less, the twenty-four-hour store I'd seen through a flickering eyelid, what seemed an eternity ago, came into view. On the corner of somewhere. I parked the rental in the car park. There was just one other car, a beaten-up Honda Civic, occupying the only other space out of a hundred or more.

***

I entered the store through two sliding electric doors. The supermarket was vast, at least the size of a football pitch. Maybe bigger. I stood still for a second under the warm air being pumped out from the heating unit directly above the doors. It felt great against my damp skin, a giant hairdryer. Inside, the light was intense compared to the shadowland where I'd been living in my previous hours. A multitude of fluorescent tubes spread confusingly across a drop ceiling, no real order, just a disarrangement of unnatural light. Their dull hum echoed in the silence that surrounded me.

Along the front of the store was a row of about ten checkouts, all of them empty apart from one. The guy glanced up at me. No real attention, just a passing glance before dipping back into his phone. His skin was dark, not black. Possibly of Indian, Pakistani, Sri Lankan, or even Indonesian descent. I could have been wrong. He had no unusual features; nothing that would make him stand out in a crowd. Late forties, medium build, grey short hair swept to one side. He wore thick-rimmed square glasses. His face was wrinkled, his forehead covered in deep lines. A tough life?

There were around half a dozen self-checkouts. The video that killed the radio star.

I picked up a basket from a stack beside me and got into the first aisle. I had a list in my head. Time was of the essence. Tick, tock, tick, tock. The cover of night my only ally.

The first six aisles were crammed with food produce – everywhere you looked, a ravenous consumer's paradise. Food was the last thing on my mind, although I hadn't eaten since noon. The sheer thought of eating made me feel sick to the stomach.

I thought back to the restaurant, the one with the black-and-yellow striped canopy, the squid from the specials board. Only yesterday, but feeling more like a week. So much had happened since then.

I shuffled down a refrigerated aisle stacked with frozen produce. The generated chill in the air ran a shiver down my spine. The CCTV above captured my every shudder.

In the next aisle, a conglomeration of tinned stuff. Tins of stuff filled with an assortment of stuff. Boxes of stuff, packets of stuff, stuff I had no fucking interest in.

A cold bead of sweat rolled down the side of my temple. I felt on edge. I must have seemed on edge. Prying eyes, big brother, CCTV documenting my fucking life. I had to keep it together. I put some eggs and bread into the basket, trying to make my presence less conspicuous. A guy returning from a nightshift, maybe. Famished and in need of a late-night omelette.

Several more aisles, still no good, my wet soles squeaking against the cheap linoleum floor beneath me as I upped the pace.

The next aisle, just an array of alcohol. Red wine, white wine, rosé wine, all split up into their own sections. Beers from around the world, spirits dark and light, the more expensive ones protected by security tags. I saw a bottle of Grey Goose, the same as the one Martin had back at his apartment. Maybe he'd bought it here.

I kept looking. An aisle full of medicine and baby products. Not what I wanted, but I picked up a box of Pro Plus, as my eyes felt like they were hanging out of my head.

I was beginning to lose my patience, the maze of the 24/7 igniting the anger within me, my blood boiling like lava. I had to keep it together. I scoped two more aisles and still nothing. I was just about to give the whole idea up, leave the store, drive back to the hostel, collect the money and see how long I could last on the run. But I didn't. I found what I was looking for.

Cleaning products. A whole aisle filled to the brim. Stacks of different shaped bottles all claiming to do the same thing better. I picked up two bottles of disinfectant, the types with the nozzle. Brilliant orange labels, bold capital letters. NO NONSENSE BLEACH. They made me think back to the cigarette in the street. What was that?

I found cleaning cloths, disposable wipes, sponge scourers, anything that could soak up the gore I had to return to. I found bin liners, the heavy-duty type, and stuffed them in the basket with everything else.

I needed one more item before I could finally get out of here. My mind was racing, and my heart was hammering in my chest.

I eventually found it. A meat cleaver. I took the last two, just to be certain, as I wasn't coming back.

I paid for my goods. The conversation between me and the guy behind the counter was non-existent. No pleasantries exchanged, just pure business.

He gave me a funny look as he scanned the meat cleavers.

Don't cause me any trouble, pal, or one of them will be hanging out the side of your head. He didn't.

I paid with cash, of course. He took my money without even a smile, as though it was my fault he was that side of the counter, my fault his life had come to this. Fuck him and his bitter pill.

The rain outside had stopped. A faint moon was now hiding behind a smoke screen of moving clouds. I got in the car and headed back to the apartment, my mind turning to Martin and his decomposing body.

In the short space of time since bludgeoning my victim to death I'd plotted out an idea in my head on how to get rid of the body. See, that was the key here. As long as I could hide his body well enough, nobody would suspect a thing, as at present I was the only person, and the last person, to have met Martin Hawker in Paris. If I could just get away with hiding the body there would be no crime, no murder scene, and in time there would be no entry in the Missing Persons' Bureau, because in time I would become Martin Hawker.

24

I pulled up outside the apartment block at precisely 1:45 am in the same spot I'd left vacant previously. I got out and made my way towards the entrance of the lobby. It was cold, the wind was hard in my face. Silence all around.

The lift ground through the shafts the same as before, the sound exaggerated in the night, putting me on edge.

I thought about the few hours ahead. Every second would count. Time was not on my side. Sunrise was about 7 am; if I was not done by then, I would be. The doors opened, I got out, I entered the apartment.

I thought about Zenith Provoski and Alberto, cold-blooded kills that I hadn't mopped up after. I hadn't really cared then – if I got caught, I got caught, I had nothing to lose – but this was different. I had the chance to start again. If I got this right I would reset my life, chuck the past in a cupboard and throw away the key.

That's why I had to make sure this was done properly, no mistakes.

I peered into the bedroom – Martin, his naked body face down on the bed, the white sheets saturated in blood. The candlestick-holder lay next to his head, the evidence of my brutality. It made it real, seeing him lying there, the obscure idea in my mind soon to be put into practice. It was now or never.

The plan was to chop Martin up into pieces, remove his limbs from his torso, his head also. It would be a grotesque task. The thought of it made me want to spew. I would then bag up the body parts, and for the remainder of the night dump then in various parts of the Seine. The Seine was over 700 kilometres in length. It covered most of Northern France. Geography was my only GCSE pass. It was my favourite lesson, but more down to Miss Temple and her great arse than my love for discovering a region.

I would drive all through the night, until dawn caught up with me, making sure each part was miles from the next. I would weigh each bag down with a dumbbell. Luckily for me Martin worked out. There was a set on the floor in his living room. I had thought at the time about caving his head in with one, but it would have looked a tad suspicious walking into the bedroom with it. The candlestick-holder had made an adequate alternative, and Martin's concaved skull was the living, or not-so-living, proof.

I believed this was the best way to make sure his body was never found. If I just dumped him whole into the river, sooner or later his decomposing corpse would float to the surface, even if it was weighted down. I wasn't an expert, obviously, but I'd seen enough TV programmes when a body had been found face down in the water. This was enough for me to go on.

I'd heard cutting through human bone was hard. A meat cleaver could easily hew small animal bones, no problem, but a human bone was a different prospect. I shuddered.

I made my way to the kitchen and emptied the contents of the bag onto the work surface. Then I began to open up one of the cleavers. It had a thick wooden handle, an alright quality. It would tear through a chicken bone with ease... but a human one?

I entered the bedroom and glanced down at Martin, his head still buried in the pillows. I rolled him over. His face was gaunt and colourless, his eyes rolled back, his mouth open.

He was in good shape – strong arms and legs, his stomach awash with abs. The dumbbells obviously weren't for show. It was a good thing I'd taken him by surprise; I reckon he would have put up a hell of a fight.

I stripped down to just my briefs, this was going to get messy.

I opened up his legs. He felt warm, as if the blood was still running through veins. I parted them as much as I could. I needed to get to his groin. This is where I would remove the legs from the torso. I could then bend his knees and bag them before rigor mortis set in. I made it sound easy, like I'd done this a hundred times before, as if chopping and bagging up human parts was a daily ritual in my life. I held the cleaver out with my left hand. My whole arm was shaking with adrenaline. Drops of sweat from my forehead splashed down on to his body as I hung over the top of him. I picked my spot, right leg first. A powerful hack would be required. I gave it everything I had.

The skin slit with ease, the blood splattering across me. I continued, hitting the same spot again, then again, then again, then again. I kept going, crashing down on the same area, over and over, not letting up, every ounce of my vitality driving through my arm.

I could see the bone now through the layers of tissue. It was like an iron bar. Every time I struck into it, the blade just ricocheted off. I must have slammed into that motherfucker fifty times, to no avail. The cleaver just wasn't strong enough. I was going to need a fucking chainsaw or an axe to get the job done.

I collapsed on my knees by the side of the bed. My arm was burning, my blood-soaked hand beginning to blister. I was in a dilemma, enervated, my whole world falling down around me. It would have been so good if I could have made it work. A chance to start again, a reincarnation, a reset.

My downfall exasperated me. I felt like running the blade of the cleaver across my wrists. What was the point in carrying on? Another murder to my name, the trail getting hotter all the time. If I left the apartment now and got away, maybe I would last for a while in the shadows of this dark world I'd created. But what would be the point of prolonging the inevitable, just to live out the next couple of months, if I was lucky, moving from one sleaze-pit to the next? Cash-only establishments, off the radar, the back streets of rundown suburbs, fraternising with the scourings of society.

Slowly, I got up off the floor, an effort, my quandary weighing me down. I'd created a blood bath, a forensics dream.

I half-heartedly thought about dumping the body in the river whole again. Who knew, I might get lucky, and it could get washed out to the English Channel undetected, chopped up in one of the propellers of a passing ferry. It was unlikely, though. Realistically he would come floating to the surface in a matter of days, the Police Nationale knocking down my door before I'd even changed the bed-sheets.

No, there had to be another way. Surely?

I'd already ruled out burying him. One, because I didn't have a shovel, and two, even if I did have one, I didn't trust the longevity of a shallow grave. No, I needed Martin to disappear off the face of the earth. But how?

I then remembered his phone. Where was it? It wasn't in the bedroom. I went back into the living room and found it on the coffee table, along with his glasses, which were folded on top of it. I tried the glasses on. Everything around me was now indistinct, a haze of confusion. It couldn't have been a more apt metaphor for how things currently stood.

25

I'd unlocked the phone with Martin's fingerprint. He didn't object. I brought up a search engine and typed in: *how do you dispose of a human corpse?*

There were 4,810,000 results in 0.49 seconds. Who was fucking writing this stuff? I started scrolling through.

There were a lot of preposterous ideas. Complete fucking kooks typing shit in abnormal post-rooms. One guy even suggested eating the corpse?!

Then I came across Robert Pickton, three pages in, halfway down, wedged between burials at sea and a story about a Brazilian woman buried alive, who'd spent eleven days trying to fight her way out of a coffin.

Robert Pickton was a psychopathic serial killer. In 2007 he was convicted of the second-degree murders of six women and was also charged with the deaths of an additional twenty women. Pickton was a former Canadian multi-millionaire pig farmer, whose victims were mostly prostitutes from Vancouver's Downtown

East side, a seedy, crime-ridden warren of cheap hotels, flop-houses, warehouses and drug dens. It was the haunt of street gangs, biker-gang members, drug dealers and pimps. Pickton, a then thirty-something eccentric, would cruise the dark streets in his open-back truck, enticing the whores back to his farm with wads of cash. Most never came back.

Pickton would later boast, after his conviction, that he'd actually killed forty-nine women and was disappointed he never made it a nice round fifty. Many prostitutes disappeared without a trace during this period, not all being tied back to Pickton.

Pickton's claims, however, led many to the conclusion that he was indeed responsible for these further missing women, and only a lack of evidence prevented justice. Pickton had confessed to an undercover officer posing as a fellow cellmate that the only reason he'd been caught was because he'd become sloppy. Up until then it had been Pickton's method of disposing of his victim's bodies that had constantly frustrated investigators. One of those methods was feeding them to the pigs.

Pigs apparently would eat almost anything, including even human bones. I narrowed the search. *Can pigs eat a whole human corpse and how long does it take?*

The first story was about a farmer from Oregon, America, who was eaten by his pigs after having a heart attack and falling into their enclosure. I also read that sixteen starved pigs could go through 200 pounds of meat in about eight minutes. Christ, those pigs could certainly eat.

I'd seen enough. I had nothing to lose. I typed in: *pig farms in Paris.*

Nothing much came up so I broadened the search. *Pig farms in France.*

It was better, obviously. I might as well have typed in pig farms around the world, there were that many. After a few minutes I narrowed it down. The closest one I could find was over 250 kilometres away in Pays de la Loire. It would take me over three hours to get there. There was no time to lose.

26

The expression 'lifting a deadweight' couldn't be more expressive. Fuck me, Martin weighed a ton. He was now sporting a trench coat, trousers and shoes. Far easier to explain why you were dragging a fully clothed man than a naked one. I'd scrubbed any traces of blood from his face and covered the laceration in his head with a cap. I'd also got rid of any visible blood on myself, changed back into my own clothes and borrowed a thick parka of Martin's, as I didn't know how long this would take. (Can you actually borrow from a dead man?)

I got out of the apartment, across the hall and into the lift. It was a struggle. I was still high on booze and my lungs were filled with smoke. A thirty-a-day habit catching up with me again. The easiest thing would have been to drag him by his arms, but I had to be prepared for the slim chance of running into someone in the middle of the night. I had his arm draped over my shoulder to give the impression I was steadying a drunk man and not a dead one. My other arm was round his waist, taking the full brunt of his weight, with his feet just dragging behind, limp and awkward.

I got out on the ground floor, Martin all fucking over me, the walking dead. I struggled across the lobby, Martin attached like a Siamese twin, legs and arms intertwined, a fucking mass of confusion.

Outside the rain was coming down with a purpose. Within the glow of the street lights dense needles of precipitation fell and splattered into the concrete pavement beneath us.

The rental was fifty yards away, sitting on the curve of the road. I approached it with caution, eyes in the back of my head. Fifty yards would feel more like fifty miles with Martin hanging ponderously on my shoulder. His hindrance was exasperating, I felt like dropping him to the ground there and then. It was lucky I didn't.

A couple ten feet ahead of me came stumbling out of an alleyway underneath the glow of a street lamp. She was a young girl, mid-twenties maybe. He was older. Much older. Someone's daughter, someone else's husband.

She was wearing a tight-fitting skirt. It was all skew-whiff, the hem riding high against her thighs. She had on tights and high boots, a white blouse and a beige camel coat. The coat was undone, the top few bottoms to her blouse open. You could see the top of her bra.

He was wearing a dark mac that was also open. I noticed the belt to his trousers was undone. He had on a pinstripe shirt that was damp and sticking to his skin. He looked in decent shape for his age. They were both wet from the rain.

We all made eye contact. She adjusted herself, pulling her skirt down and doing up her buttons. Then she wrapped her coat around her and tied it with the belt. He did the same.

Her hair was dark and short, the fringe sticking to her forehead. She was a good-looking girl from what I could work out – a slim, fresh, heart shaped face and high cheekbones. He was rugged-looking, with a tight grey haircut and good beard.

Like me they hadn't expected company at this hour. They were obviously not an item, as most couples tended to fuck within their own four walls, particularly on a night like tonight. No, he was married, a band of gold gave that away. She wore no jewellery, just slim, naked, delicate fingers.

He wrapped his arms around her petite waist. There was nothing of her. I wished Martin weighed the same. They began to come at pace towards me. He was practically dragging her, his head down, her eyes on mine. He couldn't afford to be noticed. On the other hand, she didn't give a fuck. She wanted to sing from the rooftops about them, declare her love for him in a display of public affection, carve their initials into a tree. Make love and not just screw.

His urgency to get out of the situation was to my advantage. He didn't look up once. She was more forthcoming.

'*Bon soir,*' she said as we passed, her eyes now on Martin, a confused expression.

'Forgive my friend, he's so drunk,' I said. I think she was to.

'*Anglais*?'

'*Oui.*'

She smiled, a great smile, all teeth. Great teeth, glossed plump lips, a toothpaste advert looking right at me. He hurried her past.

'*Au revoir, monsieur.*' She screamed and giggled and they disappeared into the darkness.

I'd been lucky. Very fucking lucky. I needed to get off the street. Next time I might not be as fortunate. An inquisitive bastard that would ask too many questions.

What is wrong with your friend?

He doesn't look well.

Let me take a look at him for you.

Then bang, another guy whacked, two corpses on my hands. Breakfast and lunch for my four-legged friends at my next destination.

At long last I got to the car, two minutes feeling more like two hours.

I dropped Martin onto the passenger seat, the burden off my shoulder. It felt good to stand up straight again. When I strapped him in, his head dropped forward like the corpse he'd become.

I turned over the ignition. The engine slowly rattled into life. I typed the postcode to the destination into the GPS on Martin's phone. It took several seconds for the co-ordinates to pick up, and when they did the screen told me I would be there in just over three hours. 4:14 am, to be precise.

I released the handbrake and eased out of the parking spot, checking my blind spot. All clear. No more surprises for now.

I drove for nearly three hours, I didn't know how, and I didn't know how I was still alive. I was a fucking mess – intoxicated and dangerous, my mind in and out of consciousness the whole way. I'd only stopped once, to get fuel, fags and a four-pack of Red Bull. The stimulants hadn't worked. My driving was erratic. I was all over the road, my hands constantly slipping at the wheel as sweat poured through my palms. I was too fast, then I was too slow. I straddled the centre line, next minute I was swerving onto the central reservation. I was lucky.

At this hour the motorway was near enough deserted, just the occasional juggernaut ready to crush anything in its path. I was there for the taking.

I peered at the iPhone which I'd slotted into a holder stuck to the windscreen just above the dash. The GPS told me I had 1.3 miles to my destination. It also told me I was coming off at the next junction. I slowed down, this time intentionally, then switched lanes, checking my mirrors for kamikaze truckers as I did. I hugged the inside, 50 mph, both hands tightly gripping the wheel like it was a white-knuckle ride. I felt sick, then I wanted to be. I wound down the window and threw up a gobful of bile that trickled down the side of the door. I felt hot, I felt cold, I felt hot again.

My vision was blurred. I squinted for the exit through fatigued eyes, eyes so sore and bloodshot I could almost scratch them out. I stared at myself in the rearview mirror. It would have been hard to distinguish the corpse between us.

The slip road finally lit up in the glow of my headlights. I pulled the wheel through my hands and left the motorway behind me, and was suddenly surrounded by complete darkness, a long, slow, winding lane staggered with cats' eyes that glistened like emeralds as they caught the light from my full beams.

The GPS told me 0.4 miles. I eased off the gas as

the road flicked from right to left, jolting Martin's head to face me, his eyes in the back of his head, his mouth dropped wide open.

The road grew tighter, more of a path now, the undergrowth from the dense woodland either side of me reaching out, crooked and deformed twigs grazing against the bodywork, overhanging branches blocking the glare of the moon.

With 0.1 miles to go there was a fork in the road. Two dirt tracks splitting into the horizon. The GPS told me to bear left, so I did. The surface beneath me now was plagued with potholes. The car jerked all over the place. I glanced across at Martin. He was hunched over, his head bobbing about like a nodding dog, his cap now lying upright in the footwell.

I crept ahead with caution, first gear, hardly any gas.

After bearing to the left in accordance with the graphic, the road opened up just enough for two small cars to be able to pass comfortably, with slight caution. I crawled at five miles an hour, my foot barely putting any pressure on the pedal, eyes peeled. The GPS was now telling me I was there.

I carried on. Nothing stood out, the road had become bumpy, Martin's head bobbing about even more like a nodding dog. The road ahead was straight and featureless, fields either side of me tearing away into the distance.

Nothing changed. Maybe I'd missed it? I contemplated turning around and began to doubt myself. Maybe the graphic had said bear right at the fork and not left. I was tired and my mind was stretched. Yes, that must have been it, surely? I made a turn in the road, sluggishly. The wheel felt heavy, like I was manoeuvring a tank, and not the tin can I was actually in.

The car was now straight across the road. I slammed the gear stick into reverse, and it ground into place. I wound down the window again and gazed for one last time at the road that had been ahead of me. The air was cool but not freezing, surprisingly for the time of year. A warm January day that felt like a hundred years ago was still making its mark on this dawn. I rubbed my eyes. It seemed like I' been awake for an eternity. Longer. I couldn't make anything out in the distance from the open window. I turned the wheel full lock into the direction I was facing, the tyres grinding against the loose rubble of the uneven surface below us. I eased my foot on the gas and slowly began to roll back, correcting my position, getting myself back on track. Definitely right at the fork in the road. Yes, definitely. A hundred per cent. Wasn't it?

I'd edged back as far as I could go, the undergrowth pressing up against my back window, no parking sensors. Cheap rental. I now turned the wheel full lock in the other direction, changed gear into first, foot on the gas, and made my way back in the opposite direction to the way I'd come, slowly, bumpily, the same road as before.

I'd only covered a matter of yards, had barely got into third gear, when I slammed hard on the brakes, jolting Martin forward like a crash test dummy.

I put the car into neutral and cranked up the handbrake, switched off the ignition and got out of the car.

How the fuck had I missed it?

27

The opening in the side of the road must have been around ten to twelve yards wide, a break in the undergrowth, a clear space with a decent shingle underfoot. There was a gate. Nothing fancy, ten by four foot maybe, wooden with a diamond construction. There was a hand-painted sign attached. The words *ferme porcine* dripped down the metal. The shingle continued beyond the gate, to make a straight narrow road that was lined with giant conifer trees either side, forming a perfect symmetry. At the end of the road, sitting on the horizon, the outline of a house was just visible. A light was on downstairs, a warm glow cutting through the otherwise ill-lit night.

I walked back to the car and slowly reversed into the opening, keeping my lights off. I got out and made my way round to the passenger seat, opened the door and pulled Martin out by his arms, flopping him onto the ground. Then I picked him up and moved on, through the gate and down the narrow road. I stayed close to the conifers, my cover, resting every so often.

Halfway – maybe less, fifty yards to the house at a push – I rested again, leaning back into the trunk of a tree, Martin beneath my feet, going nowhere. The house was more visible now. A rural farmhouse, with a large front-gable roof and a tall chimney that broke the skyline. White, lazy smoke spiralled up from its crown, escaping into the dead of night. The house was flat-fronted, four windows going across the top, a centralised door with two windows either side of that. A perfect symmetry.

The window with the light on was the one to the right of the door, ground floor. Maybe a hallway. Security light. Hopefully.

There was a Range Rover parked outside. Not new. The old shape before they became ultra-fashionable. It was black, I think, covered in dust, the wheel arches splattered with rust. A working vehicle, the honest toil of a farmer, not an oversized pair of Fendis to be found anywhere on the dashboard.

Rest time over. I had to get this done. I picked up Martin's arm and started to wrap it over my shoulder, but as I did so, a security light came on at the front of the house. I froze. Fuck. The light illuminated the whole drive, the Range glowing like it was in a car showroom all those years ago, nice and new and shiny. It was dark green.

I observed the house for any signs of movement. A flicker of a curtain, another light being switched on. Nothing. I put Martin down. No point wasting energy. This corpse seemed like it was getting heavier by the second. I watched. I kept on watching, crouched down like a commando over enemy lines. A murder of crows flew directly above me, their harsh cawing startling me. I watched them fly effortlessly into the distance, eventually becoming black speckles fading into the surface of the moon that was sitting on the horizon.

I turned back towards the house. It felt like it was watching me, the security light still fucking illuminating half of Paris.

Time was running out. I needed to get this done. I checked my watch. It was approaching 4:30 am. I only had a couple of hours before first light. I lit a cigarette. My mouth was bone dry, and the paper stuck to my lips. I could have drunk a river dry.

I stood up, leaving Martin at my feet, and peered out towards the house from the shadows, a stranger in the night. I pulled heavily on my Marlboro and savoured the sensation as the smoke filled my lungs.

There was still no sign of activity, no additional lights being switched on, no noise, no nothing. I took another long hard drag, then a dozen more down to its butt. I longed for another but unfortunately it was my last.

It must have been a fox or cat or something, lurking beyond the Range Rover. Whatever it was, it was still there, and I didn't have the time or patience for it to move on. I had to take a chance. To the right of the house was the silhouette of a low gate that seemed to be the entrance to some sort of track. It must of lead to the outbuildings, where I needed to get. I would have to walk across the front of the house and into the light, bringing Martin in the process. I glanced down at my corpse. The thought of dragging him again was exhausting.

I bent down, locked his armpits in my forearms and then, after a deep gulp of cold air, I began to drag him out of the shadows and into the light.

I was to the left of the house. I needed to cut across the front of it diagonally, maybe twenty yards or so, to get to the other side. Dragging the git below me, the bane of my life, was like lugging a fucking tree trunk. Awkward and agonising. I was bent in half. My spine felt like it was going to rip through my skin.

I managed to get parallel to the Range Rover, a few feet back from it. I'd moved just a few yards. It again felt more like a few miles. My arms were aching, my head was light and dizzy, like I was going to pass out. I rested for a second, trapped in the light, both of us casting long eerie shadows back down the path we'd come on. I took another deep breath, another gulp of cold air filling my lungs, giving me the inspiration to move on.

I didn't stop again, no matter how much it was hurting me. The thought of living Martin's life gave me the impetus to drive on, an inner strength burning within me. I finally reached the gate like a marathon runner crossing the line. I felt a surge of anxiety. The next half hour would determine the rest of my life.

Beyond the gate the track seemed relatively straight and I could see the outline of some buildings. Barns, warehouses, that sort of thing. I turned back towards the house. The light was still illuminating the driveway. It felt good to be back in the shadows, where I belonged. Incognito.

The distance to the outbuildings seemed at least four times as far, if not more, than the distance I'd already come. The thought of dragging Martin that far seemed impossible. There was an old tractor parked up alongside the track just ahead of me, with a trailer attached. I walked ahead to take a look, leaving Martin at the gate. He didn't mind.

The tractor was dilapidated. Even under the pale moonlight I could see its bodywork was plagued with rust, its wheel arches besmirched in thick mud, its windscreen spread with cracks that moved through the glass like giant veins.

I peered inside the trailer. I was hoping for a

217

wheelbarrow or something similar, something to dump Martin in. It was full of all sorts of shit, a tangled mess of agricultural junk. I squinted my eyes trying to make sense of a profusion of objects dusted by moonlight. Eventually I worked out there was not one single wheelbarrow... there were three! I couldn't believe my luck. I wasted no time and heaved out the one closest to me. It was heavy, Martin all over again. An encumbrance on my failing body. When I finally got it over the lip of the trailer, it crashed to the ground. The noise felt deafening. I turned back towards the house. Nothing.

I moved back to the body, bent down and, as before, locked my forearms under his armpits. Unlike before, where I just had to drag him, this time I had to physically get him into the wheelbarrow.

It took everything I had and more, and some more after that. I danced around with my corpse in the sticky mud, that sagging drunk again, all arms and legs, a fucking mass of jelly. We finally got up alongside the wheelbarrow, my forearms burning from the strain. I was weak, tired and gasping for breath. I let go of Martin's arms and let him collapse beneath me.

He crashed down in the wheelbarrow, his limbs all knotted around his torso like he was playing a one-man game of Twister. I lifted the handles, straightened my back and took a deep breath. We sluggishly advanced into the night.

The first outbuilding I came across was empty, a skeleton of corrugated iron sheets that seemed like they'd collapse in the slightest breeze. The next two buildings were much the same, disowned structures standing the test of time. The terrain beneath was now heavy. My arms felt like they were on fire. I kept going.

The fourth building was set back from the first three, a different shape, longer, newer, made of brick. There were heavy iron doors locked with a thick sturdy padlock. I thought about what could be in there. Expensive machinery, maybe? Whatever it was, it wasn't what I was looking for.

I put the wheelbarrow and Martin down just outside it, wiped the sweat from my brow and took a look around me. Before I saw it, I smelled it. Shit and mud.

Adjacent to the building, a few yards away, I could just about make out a wired fence, about waist height. I lifted the wheelbarrow. The same burning sensation shot through my arms. This had to be it, because I had nothing else left in me. I was running on empty, the mere fumes of success driving me on. As I stepped into a brand new darkness, my eyes adjusting to my new surroundings, I was elated to find that this was indeed it.

From what I could see, the sty was no more than ten by twenty yards in size, and it was most likely the first of many. Initially it appeared empty, just a pen of dense mud, but then out of the gloom they appeared, grouped together, laboriously moving as one, a mass of fat stepping towards me. Twenty or so prodigious pigs were staring at me with human-like eyes.

Fuck me, they stank. Shit and mud. They rummaged around in front of me, grunting and nudging each other to get to the front, like impatient junkies waiting on their fix. I had no time to waste.

I pulled Martin up out of the wheelbarrow by shoving my head under his arm until he slouched alongside me like the pickled mess I'd made him out to be earlier.

Forgive my friend, he's so drunk

We danced towards the fence, my friend and I, an uncoordinated tango, our final embrace. Once we reached the fence I stood him up alongside it, then slowly lowered my hands down his arms, across his biceps, over his elbows and onto his wrists.

He began to tilt backwards, his torso arching across the fence. He hung from my hands like a schoolchild playing with his parents in the playground.

A parent, however, would never let go. I most definitely did. Martin collapsed back into the sty, hitting the ground with an almighty thud that seemed to echo forever into the night. The pigs backed off. The corpse lay awkwardly, face down in the mud, his limbs at acute angles.

Nothing happened. The herd just looked on inquisitively. Maybe my hogs weren't hungry. Maybe the phenomenon of humans being eaten by pigs was actually bollocks. I took a step back, ready to run.

'Eat, goddam it,' I screamed, not caring how far my voice travelled. 'Come on, eat, you filthy bastards! Eat!'

My world was collapsing around me. I made to light a smoke but remembered I'd smoked my last. Jesus, give us a fucking break. I turned my back on the sty and gathered my bearings for the way back. At least it would be easier without Martin hindering my every move. If there was ever a time to smoke, this was it. I would buy some for the journey. Where I was going, I didn't know.

I looked back one final time. It was not how Martin would have liked to have been remembered, his face buried in shit and mud. An impertinent ending to one's life. I made to turn my back on him for the last time, but as I did so, one of the hogs suddenly broke from the herd and began poking its leathery snout into the corpse's head. The others began to follow, rummaging around the body, seeing what was on offer. I watched intently, staying where I was, a few feet from the fence, dead still, dead quiet, so I didn't spook them. Then it happened, just like that.

The first pig, the leader of the pack, was a wide

sturdy creature that swaggered about like he was the boss. No one would make a move until he did, and he did, savagely biting into Martin's cheek with a violent and blistering force. It was like ringing the dinner bell. The others moved in.

It must have taken about fifteen minutes. Maybe more, maybe less. I watched every bite, every mouthful, until Martin Hawker was no more, apart from inside my head.

Those pigs could certainly eat.

28

The week went by in a flash. It was now Sunday, the night before I was due to start work at Regnard and Son's. Well, Martin was due to start, to be precise.

I'd done so much in such a short space of time. The apartment looked great. Not a trace of the murder that had only happened a week ago. It had stood the test of time, too, when the landlady had turned up unannounced on the Wednesday. She was a short, stubby woman, around seventy, with grey, unkempt, frizzy hair. She introduced herself as Magdalene Bernhardt, I introduced myself as Martin Hawker. Her English was very broken, but we managed to come to an understanding that the rent would be paid at the start of each month, and that she would prefer cash. The arrangement suited me just fine. She'd brought me a *galette des rois* which she said she'd baked herself. It was very good. Magdalene would be no trouble.

I bought myself some clothes from a local tailor

in a quirky back street, about five minutes from the apartment. It had the added bonus of having a cute café next door which made the most wonderful cappuccinos. I'd found myself most mornings in the past week sitting outside this café, nursing fresh coffee and smoking. I am sure it was what Martin would have done. Wouldn't he?

Along with some white crisp shirts, ties and shoes I bought a couple of suits. One was navy, and one was a light grey, with a waistcoat. I particularly liked the grey one as it reminded me of the suit Sean Connery wore in *Goldfinger*.

I took the car rental back without a hitch and enquired about further rentals. I thought it might be nice to get out of Paris the occasional weekend without looking over my shoulder. The French Riviera, maybe.

I'd dyed my hair bleach blonde and bought glasses like Martin's, but with plain lenses. I'd also purchased a bundle of non-prescription coloured contact lenses from the internet. Pale blue, as close to Martin's as I could remember. Although Martin had said he hadn't really met anyone, who knew who had seen him come and go from his apartment? I had to look as much like him as I could. I also had to look as little like me as possible. I'd been all over the papers, with CCTV footage from the hotel.

One headline from the *Le Figaro* read: *Eventreur de*

Londres en Liberté.

This translated as *London Ripper on the Loose.* There was also a clear picture.

I also had to pass for Martin's passport photo, since Alfredo's email had stated I needed to bring it on my first day. That would be the biggest hurdle yet, but that was Monday's problem, and tonight I wouldn't dwell on the possibility of this meticulous plan failing.

I'd booked a table at La Cabane Mussel for 7:30 pm, a restaurant I'd read good things about on a review website. It wasn't far from the apartment, a ten-minute stroll, tops. I wore the navy suit jacket but with jeans and an open-neck shirt. One of Martin's. It fitted OK.

At 7:15 I was ready to leave for what could possibly be my last meal as a free man. If they didn't fall for the passport, I'd give myself up there and then. Wouldn't I?

Before I left, I took out Martin's passport. It was in a box in the wardrobe, along with the money I'd gone back to the hostel for on the morning I left the pig farm.

I went into the bathroom and stood in front of the mirror, holding the passport alongside my face. There was a resemblance. It could just be good enough to pass the inspection at the office.

'Hi, I'm Martin Hawker,' I said to the blonde in the mirror.

'It's a pleasure to meet you,' the reflection replied.

29

La Cabane Mussel was as good as they'd said. I had the scallops to start with, followed by a delightful piece of seabass, all washed down with a good Sauvignon.

I left the restaurant around 9:30. The evening crowd was just getting going, with all the ambience of a Sunday night in Paris. I ambled home, stopping off for a quick nightcap in a small but busy bistro called Raphaël's.

Raphaël's was situated on the corner of a cobbled crossroads about a quarter of a mile from my apartment. It was en route to the main drag in to town, about twenty minutes by foot to the Avenue des Champs-Élysées. It would be a walk I would soon be familiar with, as the office was just off the avenue on a small back street housing half a dozen office blocks. Door to door it would take just over thirty minutes. I'd done it once using Google maps. I remembered thinking at the time that Raphaël's would be a nice place to stop on the way home occasionally, to sip on an ice-cold beer on a balmy summer's evening and watch the world go by from one of the round tables scattered on the pavement outside. The tables looked inviting, each one decorated with a vase and fresh flowers, each one draped in an immaculate white tablecloth that had been pressed with loving care and attention.

Tonight was anything but a balmy summer's evening. The air was cool, but it was a nice clear night, stars glittered across the sky like far away diamonds.

The bistro was split between two streets – a small alleyway and the main drag, with the alleyway running adjacent to the main drag but pulling away slightly at a rough forty-five-degree angle. The main entrance was at the vertex – or the pointy bit, to the less geometry-minded. There were two large sash windows either side, facing out onto both streets. A multitude of square glass panes were held together by worn timber glazing bars that needed a fresh lick of paint. Both windows, and the main entrance, were covered with cherry red canopies.

I lit a smoke before I went in, taking in the evening around me. My cigarette tasted exquisite, the first one after a meal always did. As I contemplated lighting another, something grabbed my attention. Laughter from above. I stepped out from the canopy and peered up.

Further up the bistro there was a black wrought-iron balcony that stretched around the perimeter of the building, outside an apartment, exactly the same square feet as the restaurant but over two floors, possibly three. It was hard to tell from the ground and at night.

Beyond the balcony were two double doors, looking out to the heart of the City. A good spot, I thought. A1 real estate.

A youngish couple were sitting outside at a table, outlined against the warm pale glow of the apartment beyond them.

They sounded like they were living life to the full as they sipped on wine, smoked and gazed out into the night. What a great place to live, I thought, as I stumped my own cigarette out on the cobbled street below.

We don't have anything for dinner, do we, darling? Let's go down to the bistro. I think we're out of wine, darling. Let's go down to the bistro. Parfait.

I smiled to myself and stepped into the bistro for the first time. Inside, it was warm. The square, individual panes of the sash windows were steamed up, the outside world blurred by a mass of condensation.

I found a seat at the bar and asked if it was OK to have just a drink, as the seabass was still lining my stomach. It wasn't a problem. I ordered a large brandy – the good stuff, and not the local produce they passed off to tourists. I'm a local now.

The bistro was a decent size, ten tables maybe, each

one occupied. I took it in, minding my own business, just happy to sit in silence and not having to make conversation with anybody. I thought about Monday and what it could bring, a new life, a new start. I thought about the passport, everything riding on it.

I ordered one for the road, same again, same glass. I briefly spoke with the guy who'd served me, an old gentleman, the proprietor I imagined, by the way he spoke to the other staff. He asked if I was on holiday. I filled him in. Not every detail but the gist of it. As I was leaving I told him I'd be back. He shook my hand and gave me an affectionate smile.

'What's your name?' he said.

'Martin. And yours?'

'François. *Au revoir, monsieur* Martin.'

'*Au revoir*, François.'

Outside, the stars had vanished behind a developing fog, as along with the laughter from the balcony above. I looked up. The young couple were no longer there, just two vacant seats and a round table with an empty wine bottle on it.

I thought about how they would probably be fucking right now, her on top, plenty of noise. It made me smile. It turned me on.

I started to make my way back to the apartment. There was a chill in the air. I turned up the collar on my jacket. I couldn't wait to get into my warm bed, a good night's sleep before the big day ahead. I would think of the young couple one more time, however, before doing so.

30

Monday – 8:25 am.

I left for work in plenty of time. I was wearing the grey suit, the one like James Bond in *Goldfinger*, and a white shirt and black tie. 007, licence to kill.

I passed Raphaël's around 8:40. François was outside, placing fresh flowers on the tables.

'*Bonjour, monsieur* Martin.'

'*Bonjour*, François.'

'Your first day. Good luck. Very smart,' he said, tugging at his apron.

'Thank you and *au revoir*. I'll pop by on my way home for a drink,' I said over my shoulder, as I disappeared into the next street.

'Why, of course!' he hollered.

I arrived at the office at 9:05. Too early. Alfredo had distinctly said 9:30, so I found myself a café and sat outside. It was a nice bright morning and the sun felt almost warm.

I ordered a cappuccino from an elderly guy who looked about a hundred and moved in slow motion. I didn't order any food. As much as the pastries in the window appeared delightful, my stomach was doing somersaults.

The café was in the next street to the firm. By 9:25 I'd paid with a tip and was walking to the office, with a Marlboro smouldering between my fingertips.

Regnard et fils was on the second floor, wedged between a publisher's and consultancy firm on the intercom system. The small name tag was written by hand in biro, not printed up fancy like the others, but it was neat and served its purpose.

I pressed the buzzer and waited. After a few seconds a woman's voice crackled out from the intercom.

'*Bonjour, Regnard et fils*?'

'*Monsieur* Hawker, I believe you are expecting me?'

'*Oui, monsieur* Hawker. Please pull the door.'

The door clicked. I opened it and stepped into a small square lobby. Inside the carpet was worn. It smelled damp. The walls, painted in magnolia, were drab and needed freshening up.

Against the back wall there was a flight of stairs, to the right a single lift shaft, to the left a desk covered in dust and scattered with junk mail. I imagined how it used to be, occupied by an old security guard, peaked cap and blazer, full of conversation. He would sign you in, escort you to the lift. Service with a smile. How it should be but now replaced with an intercom system. Some cost-cutting exercise by a bunch of fucking weasels at head office who didn't give a shit about people's lives.

I took the lift, pressed number two and the door shut. The wires cranked into place and up I slowly went. I felt hot, I felt sick, I felt nervous. I loosened my tie. I was suddenly gasping for air. Shit, this was it.

The door finally opened to a reception area – two desks with a frosted glass panel behind them – and beyond that the buzz of a nine to five. I pictured it in my head – people hard at it, bums on seats, eyes firmly fixed on screens, phones wedged under chins and the weekend nothing but a distant memory.

There was only one receptionist. The other desk was empty. A tea break or maybe another victim of the weasels.

'*Bonjour,* Mr Hawker,' she said. '*Bonjour.*'

She got up from her desk and greeted me with a soft handshake. Her skin was warm, like she'd been nursing a hot cup of coffee, waiting for something to happen. My hand must've felt like shit. Wet and clammy.

She was about sixty, give or take, with natural grey hair, short and respectable. A pair of glasses hung from a chain around her neck. Convenient. She was wearing a plain blouse and knee-length skirt. She had a good figure for her age.

'I am Gabriella. It's a pleasure to meet you. Please take a seat. May I get you tea or coffee?'

'Coffee would be great, thank you.' It would be my fourth of the morning, but who was counting?

'White, black, latte, cappuccino?'

'Cappuccino would be great.'

'Sugar?'

'No, thanks.'

She disappeared through a door in the glass panel behind the desks. I got a glimpse of my new world before it swung shut behind her. *Nine to five.*

She reappeared about a minute later holding a plastic cup. Coffee from a machine. We both sat down and got acquainted. Nothing too heavy, just shooting the breeze. The coffee was adequate.

Gabriella's English was flawless.

'OK, let's get you started. Before I show you to your desk, do you have your passport?'

'Sure.'

I pulled the passport from the pocket in my suit jacket. This was it, the moment of truth.

'Great, I'll just take a copy.'

She took the passport off me, walked over to a large photocopier in the corner and lifted the lid. She opened my passport to the page with my details and photo, but instead of laying it on the glass top to copy, she hesitated. She put on the glasses that hung around her neck and stared hard at the open page. Then she took them off and glared hard over at me.

My heart sank.

'It's an old photo,' I said, my voice all squeaky from a sudden dry throat.

'One moment.' Gabriella raised her finger as she spoke, like a school teacher putting a pupil in place.

She shut the lid to the machine, made her way over to her desk and picked up the phone. She dialled a number from memory. Four digits. Internal.

This was it, the end of the road. I suddenly felt hot. Fucking boiling. Sweat seeping out of my body at such a rate, it was as if the pores in my skin were the size of manholes. Who was she calling? Security? Maybe she was going straight to the police? I'd thought the number was internal, but maybe she needed to get an outside line by dialling nine first then 999 for emergency services, or whatever the French equivalent was.

It wouldn't take them long to find out who I really was. They would raid the flat and eventually come across my own passport hidden in the secret compartment I'd made in one of the bedroom drawers. I should have burnt it, chucked it down a drain, or left it in Martin's shirt pocket for the pigs to devour. But I didn't. For some reason I needed to keep it, a reminder to myself from time to time of who I really was. If this preposterous scheme had ever succeeded, I'd have liked to occasionally get the passport out. Not often, maybe once a year as an anniversary, or something daft like that. I would have a little drink to myself, a toast to who I once was. I found the thought warming, mainly because it would have meant I was getting away with it, the quintessential blueprint to stealing another man's identity.

That notion was quickly squashed, like a fly on a wall. Gabriella finally got through. I froze, my heart beating so fast it felt as if I had to push down on my chest to stop it erupting through my skin. I was nauseous, my mouth watery, that feeling you get when you know you're just about to spew your guts up. I didn't, though. I don't know how.

She spoke very briefly, in French of course, a jumble of words slipping off the tongue, fast, smooth, precise. The only thing I picked up on was my name. She'd mentioned *Monsieur* Hawker once, for sure, but before the call ended she sounded out my full name, slowly. I pictured the person on the other end writing it down. *Martin Alexander Hawker.*

'OK.'

'OK.'

'*Merci.*'

She put the phone back on the receiver. I gulped.

'Sorry about that. I didn't realise you had a middle name. I was just giving it to Michelle. She deals with payroll and it makes life easier if we put all the correct details down. Right, let me get this copied, then we can get you started.'

I couldn't believe it. It had worked. It had fucking worked. I wanted to jump up, dance around the room, grab Gabriella by the shoulders and kiss her a hundred times on each cheek. I didn't, of course. I just sat there in a daze, dreaming of what was to come. A new start, a new life, a new person.

'Martin?'

I didn't know how long Gabriella had been calling my name but she was standing by the door to the office, waiting for me to follow her.

'Sorry, day dreaming. Big day. Slightly nervous and all that.' I got to my feet.

'Totally understandable. Take your time.'

I dusted myself down and tightened the knot in my tie. I took a long, deep breath. 'Ready.'

31

The moment Alfredo Regnard appeared on the office floor the mood changed dramatically. Bums got back on seats, heads went down and the general chit-chat of the weekend fizzled out with every footstep as he glided gracefully through the maze of desks to his own private office. He didn't look at me once, not even the faintest glance, but I knew it was him. I just felt it.

I'd spent some of the morning being introduced to people and getting the office tour by a guy whose name I'd already forgotten. Toilets, coffee area, stationery, fire exits, all the usual standard bullshit. Yawn. When was lunch?

The rest of the morning I sat at my new desk, knee-deep in a starter pack that could have given the Bible a run for its money. Read this, sign that, tick the box, don't tick the fucking box. Yawn. When was lunch?

At 1:40 pm I was into my third cup of mediocre coffee from the vending machine when the phone rang, startling me.

'Hello, Martin speaking.'

'Martin, Alfredo. Please come to my office.'

Alfredo had a glass-panelled office towards the back of the floor, away from the workforce, the only one of its kind. When I approached the door was ajar, a basic wood-panelled door with his name across it in bold italics. Alfredo was on another call, feet on desk, arched back in his leather chair. He waved me in, pointed to one of the chairs opposite him and then gestured with his finger that he would only be a minute. I took a seat and waited.

His office was basic and understated. A beige metal filing cabinet to his left, around waist-height. A small potted green plant on top that was in desperate need of watering. A canvas on the wall, a print – the Eiffel Tower in a splash of watercolours, one of many similar. His desk was bare. A telephone and laptop, a silver picture frame facing towards him. Kids, wife, probably. There was a coat-stand in the corner, a single trilby hanging by its rim and a black trench coat. The window behind him had a Persian blind pulled down, the horizontal slats covered in dust rotated ninety degrees to let in the natural light that shone on Alfredo's head and emphasised his receding hairline.

He was still on the phone, occasionally glancing over

at me and rolling his eyes. One minute became five, and then five became ten.

When the call finally ended fifteen minutes later, Alfredo jumped up out of the chair and greeted me with both hands, like an old friend he hadn't seen for years.

'Martin, it is a pleasure to at long last put a name to a face.'

'Likewise. It's a pleasure to meet you, Mr Regnard.'

'Please, call me Alfredo. Now, first things first. Have you eaten?'

'Well, I was going to grab a sandwich from the café on the corner.'

'Sandwich!' He laughed profusely. 'Grab your jacket. I'm taking you to Alexandre's at once.'

32

Alexandre's was buzzing for a Monday. A nice weekend hangover cure.

The restaurant was grand. Marble floors and mirrored walls, vast exquisite chandeliers hanging from high ceilings painted like something out of the Sistine Chapel. The tables were round, with ivory satin tablecloths, fifty to sixty covers maybe, most of them taken. The chairs were oak, covered in the finest leather, heavy and bold, and more like armchairs, the type you could sink into and never want to leave.

Alfredo was met with open arms by the maître d', a middle-aged, grey-haired, distinguished-looking gentleman in a full penguin suit, bow tie, waistcoat – the whole nine yards. Clean-cut and handsome, the sort of guy you would want fronting your restaurant. Yes, he was incredibly good-looking. He had this amazing hair, long and wavy, effortlessly pushed back off of his face. His teeth sparkled, his skin was tanned like he'd had just got off a plane from some exotic destination.

Alfredo introduced me as Mr Hawker. I liked that. It made me feel important, like I was someone. The guy's name was Michel. They exchanged pleasantries for a bit. Michel's voice was deep and enchanting. Why, he could make beans on toast sound like caviar and quails' eggs.

We were eventually shown to a table – a cute table for two in the centre of the restaurant. I was right about the chairs. Wild horses wouldn't be able to drag me out.

'Are you a steak man?' Alfredo asked, as he adjusted the cutlery and made himself comfortable.

Hell, yeah, I was. Why, right now I could eat a whole fucking cow. 'Love steak.'

'Of course you do, I knew it. Alexandre's does the best steaks this side of Paris. *Beau!*' He kissed his fingers.

'Great,' I said. Who was I to argue?

A waiter approached, young, spotty straight out of high school. He was extremely thin and tall, size twelve shoes at least. He could practically have hidden behind a golf club. He wore a white shirt and black tie underneath a smart waistcoat. No jacket. His sleeves were rolled up neatly above his elbows, his arms long and dangly, like a chimpanzee's.

'*Bonjour.*' He made to hand us both a menu, but Alfredo stopped him.

'*Parles-tu anglais?*' he asked.

'Yes, *monsieur.*'

'Excellent. My friend here is still learning the language, so it would be nice for him to be involved.'

'Of course.'

'Right, we don't need any menus. Can you tell chef Dubuque Monsieur Regnard would like to see him, please?'

'Yes, sir.'

'André, the head chef, is a personal...' He paused. 'Sorry, one moment.' He turned and called to the waiter, who had barely left the table. He walked back over, his body language spritely and energetic, like nothing could ever be a problem.

'Wine?' Alfredo asked, looking across the table at me.

'Yes.'

'White?'

'Love white.'

'Excellent.' He spoke to the waiter. 'That little vineyard in the Loire Valley, along the river from Pouilly-sur-Loire.'

'Saint–Andelain, *monsieur,*' the waiter said, without hesitation.

'Ah, that's it!' Alfredo clicked his fingers.

'The '67 of course, *monsieur.*'

'Excellent.'

The boy turned away and Alfredo turned his attention back to me again. 'The '67 is an honest little wine, especially if you let it breathe a bit. It has a fresh and crisp flavour made from the Chasselas grape. I think you will like it.'

'I'm sure I will.'

'I'm not a believer that the wine should match the food, Martin, are you?'

'Er…'

'I love white wine, I love steak. So why can't I have them together?'

'Beats me.'

'That business with the waiter, making him and me speak in English. I hope you don't think I was being… What's the word? Supercilious? Have you had any lessons yet?'

I thought about the book on the coffee table, *Fluent in Three Months*. I'd browsed through the pages, nothing more.

'I have my first lesson with a tutor on Wednesday,' I said. 'A woman named Sophia. Does home tutoring.'

A big fat lie. I'd told so many now I was actually starting to believe them myself.

'Very good. Or should I say "*Très bien*". That one is for free.'

I laughed. '*Très bien*,' I said.

'*Parfait.*'

'You mentioned something about the chef?' I said, gazing round the restaurant, in awe of it all.

'Ah, yes, André. He's a personal friend of mine and an excellent chef. Ah, here he comes now.'

Alfredo greeted the man, dressed in white head-to-toe, same as Michel. The big embrace and all that jazz.

We were introduced. Mr Hawker again. Nice touch. They then chatted in English for my benefit, chewing the fat, almost literally, as they discussed different cuts of meat. Finally it was decided we were having the *filet mignon* from a cow that had been grain-fed for 400 days. The meat had then been wet-aged for thirty days and then dry-aged for ten days. Again, who was I to argue?

Alfredo finished with some light conversation with the chef – how's the family, blah, blah, blah. Fuck the family. Let the man go and get my steak on.

I sat there quietly, of course, with a half-smile on my face, listening like I gave a shit about a stranger's wife and two kids. So far I had, however, enjoyed watching Alfredo go about his business – the way he spoke to people, cool, calm and collected, a real swagger to his manner, the man about town.

Alfredo was probably mid- to late-sixties, receding long black hair gelled back tightly to his scalp. His complexion was swarthy, his nose was long and pointy.

He was slightly overweight but by no means obese. His black tailored suit, with a white chalk pinstripe running through it, was matched with a carnation pink shirt which rocked monogrammed cuffs. He was wearing a gold watch. Patek Philippe. His hands were darkly tanned, like his face. Darker, in fact. A real sickly brown, like he'd dipped them in a tin of wood-stain. They looked soft, as though he'd never done a hard day's work. His fingers were short and stubby, his fingernails immaculate. He wasn't wearing a wedding ring; he wasn't wearing any rings at all.

The wine eventually arrived with a smile, a cute blonde breaking my train of thought. Alfredo gestured to the waitress that I should try the wine while he said his goodbyes to André. She was no more than a girl – twenty at a push, fresh and trim, everything in the right places. She poured a small drop into my cut-crystal glass, which was glistening in the sunlight that had suddenly spread across the restaurant. I took a sip. Alfredo was right. I did like it. The '67, of course.

33

The food had come and gone. The steaks were fucking mind-blowing. *Beaux*!

We'd sat talking for two hours – the job, me, him and Ruby. It was lucky Martin had gone into such detail about her; I could act as though I really knew her. The restaurant had thinned out – that time between lunch and dinner, just a few dribs and drabs nursing their brandies.

'Right, time stands for no man, Martin. I'm on the red eye into JFK tonight. Business, of course. I'll settle up and will have to be on my way. Listen, it's nearly four o'clock. Don't worry about going back to the office. Not much point now. Get yourself home, enjoy your evening and start afresh tomorrow.'

'If you're sure?'

'Of course I'm sure. Now, where's my wallet?'

Alfredo shuffled about in his suit pockets. He stood up, padded down his trousers and then repeated the whole process again, and then again. It was that thing that we all do – you lose something but keep checking the same place over and over, even though you know it's not there. Human nature.

'I must've left it in the office.'

'Please, let me pay.' I took some cash from my inside pocket.

'Put your money away, Martin, this is on me. Plus, what are expenses for, right?'

He gave a laugh that was more of a snigger. I'd seen it all before – brokers back in the City, London another time. Client lunches and dinners, a few drinks after work, all run through the firm's black American Express.

'I'll call my secretary to bring it down. She can also get my car, save me having to go back to the office. I still need to pack and Paris can be a bitch in the rush hour.'

He made his call, quick and to the point, a few seconds to get the message across, this time in French and not for my benefit. He asked for the bill and then we waited. Alfredo fiddled with his phone, browsing emails as I drank the last of the '67 slouched in the chair I would never leave. I felt wonderful.

It must have been no more than five minutes before she stepped into the restaurant. She came straight over to our table and handed Alfredo a set of car keys and a black crocodile-skin wallet.

'Martin, I would like you to meet Zelia. Zelia,

Martin Hawker started at the firm today. Well, sort of, eh, Martin?'

Alfredo winked at me and raised his glass.

I got up from the chair I would never leave and shook her soft hand. From that moment I was hooked, like a junkie to a crack pipe. Zelia was early thirties, no more. Light brown short hair with a side parting that was neatly kept in place by a slide. Her eyes were hazel, her skin fair. She had these amazing cheekbones and voluptuous Cupid's bow lips that screamed out for kisses. There was a cute cluster of freckles across the bridge of her nose and a very faint beauty spot on the corner of her mouth. She wore very little make-up, if any at all. She didn't need it. A tight-fitting black knee-length dress hung from her size ten figure just fine. All the curves in the right places. A suit jacket hung over her shoulders. A quick dash from the office. She smelled fucking wonderful.

As our hands parted, I could not help but notice the dent in her wedding finger. A divorcee? It was too good to be true, wasn't it?

Alfredo chucked down a bit of plastic onto the table – black American Express, obviously – breaking the moment. Had there been a moment?

A waiter attended to the bill. Not one I'd seen all afternoon. Here for the night shift but picking up the pieces from the final stragglers at lunch.

We all left together. Outside the late afternoon sky had turned a mystical blood orange as the sun dipped beneath the buildings to the west, casting long solid shadows on the streets below us.

'Right, this is me,' Alfredo said. He clicked the fob in his hand, lighting up a Maserati parked across the street. He shook my hand. '*Au revoir*, Martin. I will see you next week, when I'm back in the country.'

'Yes, and thank you for such a wonderful lunch.'

'No problem. As I said, what are expenses for? *Au revoir*, Zelia.'

He walked across the road and got into the car. Its roar echoed through the street as he revved the throttle.

The sun had all but disappeared, dipping out of Paris and lighting up another time-zone with its glorious rays, a warm sunny morning somewhere far away. Zelia and I stood in silence after the car had gone, strangers in the street brought together by a mutual party. The street lights slowly flickered on all around us. Paris by night. I thought of the watercolour back in Alfredo's office. I couldn't see the Tower from where I stood, but I imagined it now, looking as it did in the picture.

I broke the silence. Someone had to.

'OK, then. Well, I guess I'll see you tomorrow in the office. Unless… No, don't worry.'

'Unless what?'

'Unless... Unless you fancied coming for a quick drink?'

My heart skipped a beat. Fuck, what had I done? If she said no – of course she'd say no, without doubt she'd say no – I'd live to regret it. There would be moments, plenty of moments, when our paths would cross in a deserted corridor, or when the difficult playout would be just us two in the lift. Fuck, I'd have to take the stairs for life. I wished I could turn back time. One minute ago from now. Say, 'Goodbye,' and, 'I'll see you around.' Get the fucking hell out, with my pride intact.

Come on, Zelia, put me out of my misery. Tell me thanks but no thanks, and let me disappear into the darkness with my tail between my legs.

She finally spoke. It had seemed an eternity but in reality seconds. 'I'd like that.'

'That's OK,' I said. 'Right, well, I'd better be going before—'

She interrupted me. 'I said I would like that, Martin.'

'Oh, right. OK, great.'

'Let me go and finish off. I'll meet you at a bar in the next street called The Polo Club, you can't miss it. Not all of us get the big boss's approval to leave early for the day.'

I blushed. We both stood looking at each other. We both smiled. The world stood still, and for a few seconds it felt like there was only us in it. Back in the restaurant I'd thought there may have been a moment. I could have been wrong. I often was. But if there wasn't… Goddam, if there wasn't, there definitely was one now.

34

Six months later

My instructions that evening had been clear: pick up some wine and don't be late. There was no mention of don't stop at Raphaël's. That I did.

It was a beautiful afternoon, sunny and warm. I'd left the office at 3:30 and picked up a few bottles of the Pinot Noir we liked. I then made time for a quick drink. A gin and tonic sitting outside Raphaël's would do just nicely. Very nicely indeed.

I sat at a round table at the edge of the bistro. The sun was on my face. It felt great, just like my life did. I had everything I wanted and more.

I drained the remains of my second gin and tonic and set off for home, which was now a two-bedroom apartment with a beautiful south-facing balcony, only a few streets away from my previous dwelling. It had felt good to get out of Martin's place, finally burying the past and starting afresh. When Zelia suggested we should move in together – we were practically living together anyway – I was ecstatic.

We'd only picked the keys up two weeks ago. Everything since then had been so hectic, our feet not touching the ground. So tonight we were going to celebrate properly, toast our new home over a good meal and a few glasses of wine. It had all been planned. Zelia had taken the afternoon off to prepare the meal. She'd also let slip that she'd stopped off and bought some new lingerie. She knew how to entice me, make sure I was home on time and not distracted too much. The sex was amazing. Nothing was off the table.

I reached the apartment at 5 pm. Zelia was in the kitchen cooking bouillabaisse, her pièce de résistance. It smelled fucking great, as did she as she approached and kissed me on the lips. She tasted as good as she smelled.

I held her in my arms and gazed at the apartment over her shoulder. It was still pretty much upside down. Unpacked boxes everywhere, half-stripped walls flecked with various shades of paint while we debated on the colour scheme.

The apartment was a good size. We were on the top floor of a three-storey building. Zelia called it the penthouse. Not quite, as we shared the floor with Monsieur Truffaut, an elderly gentleman who lived opposite us and who always wore a suit. He was eighty-five, he'd proudly told me. He had a thick mop of grey hair and his own teeth. Something else he'd also told me.

There was a square entryway as you walked into the apartment. Just off of this, and diagonal to the front door, was the entrance to the kitchen, which ran parallel to the living room, from which it was separated by a stud wall. Beyond the living room was a small corridor with two bedrooms and a bathroom running off it. The bedrooms were of equal size, so we chose the one that gave us a view of the Eiffel Tower (just!).

At the bottom of the kitchen there was a small scullery with patio doors leading out to the great south-facing balcony. We'd bought some rattan furniture and a patio heater and had spent most of our time out there since we moved in. It was an excellent space. We would drink wine and watch the sun go down. *De toute beauté*! (*Fluent in Three Months* was paying off.)

'So what are we drinking?'

I took one of the bottles of Pinot Noir from the box I'd placed on the side and held it aloft.

'Our favourite.'

'Great. Well, get it open, then.'

I pulled open a drawer and took out a corkscrew – one of the old-fashioned types, just a wooden perpendicular handle with a metallic helix coiling from it. I opened the bottle and twisted the cork off the screw, then smelled it, inhaling deeply.

'Why do you always sniff the cork, Mr Hawker, like you know what you're doing?'

Zelia's facetious remark was followed by a tantalising grin. She was lolling against the kitchen units alongside me, the wooden spoon in her hand coated in the sauce from the bouillabaisse. She was wearing a simple white dress that sat just above the knee. She'd bought it in a charity shop, but she looked a million dollars in it. That was Zelia all over. She didn't need designer clothes, shoes or handbags; she looked good in practically anything. I glanced down at her legs, slender and tanned, her feet bare, her toenails painted pink. I poured the wine, still ogling the woman in front of me. I could fuck her right now.

'There you go, Miss Sarcastic. And for your information, I do know what I'm doing. I'm sniffing to detect cork taint, which can tell you if the wine itself is corked, without you having to taste it.'

'You've been spending far too much time with François.' She took a sip. 'But well done. The wine is excellent.'

I gave her a slap on the arse. 'Cheeky cow. How long till dinner?'

'Half an hour, and ouch!'

'Half an hour? Maybe that gives us some time for me

to check out this new lingerie.'

I moved in close behind her, wrapping my arms around her waist, brushing my face against hers.

'This bouillabaisse needs my undivided attention, Monsieur Hawker, unfortunately. But don't worry, the dessert will be phenomenal.'

We kissed, our mouths slightly open, our tongues tenderly touching.

'Are you sure we don't have time?' I said, pulling away from her slightly.

'It will be worth the wait, trust me.'

Zelia stepped back and lifted her dress up past her waistline. She was wearing a red lace thong, hardly anything to it. It had two bows at the front holding it all together. I imagined just pulling them open and letting it fall to the floor.

'Agent Provocateur,' she whispered, like there were other people in the room.

I made to touch her, but she stopped my advancing hand with hers, grabbing my wrist and holding it tight. She pulled me towards her, putting her lips against my ear. 'Do you want to fuck me?'

My dick was like a rocket in my pants. I wanted to push her up against the wall and come inside her.

'Yes. I want you so bad.'

She grabbed at my erection. 'Yes, you do, don't you?'

I made to unfasten my belt, but for the second time she stopped me in my tracks.

'Later,' she said, moving back to the hob and stirring the bouillabaisse.

'You little bitch,' I said, with a smirk.

She laughed and blew me a kiss. 'All good things come to those who wait, my darling.'

She had me hook, line and sinker. This fish was well and truly caught.

'Right, in that case I'm going for a cigarette, Mademoiselle Prick-Tease.'

'Why, monsieur, such appalling allegations.'

We both laughed, and I picked up my wine and stepped outside.

The weather was still glorious, every square foot of the balcony bombarded with sunrays. I sat down and undid a few buttons on my shirt, took my glasses off and closed my eyes. The warm air wrapped itself around me like an invisible blanket. I instantly felt relaxed, at ease. My arms slowly unfolded away from my body, my legs splayed out beneath me. I titled my head back and let the sun kiss my forehead, feeling myself drift away as my fingers loosened around the stem of the wine glass. I began to dream.

It felt like I'd been out for hours when I was suddenly rudely awakened by Zelia. She had shoved an ice cube down my shirt. I shot up like I was being executed from an electric chair. She was standing in front of me, blocking the sun.

'I'll get you for that,' I said, lighting the cigarette I'd actually gone out to smoke in the first place. I checked my watch. I'd only been out for five minutes.

'Anyway, what are you doing out here? I thought your bouillabaisse required your undivided attention.'

'It does, my darling, but I thought you could make yourself useful, seeing as I'm slaving over a hot stove for you. I thought you could maybe book the flights to Rome?'

Rome had been on the agenda for the past couple of weeks. A city break, just a few days to get away. We both had time off work owing to us, and it had always been a dream of Zelia's to visit the Vatican City. I was more up for a relaxing break. A few days lazing around a pool somewhere seemed much more appealing. The Costa Brava, the Algarve, even the South of France. But Zelia had her heart set on Rome. She spoke about it so passionately, and I for one wasn't going to argue, as long as the next holiday involved me floating around on a lilo somewhere sipping on ice-cold beers.

'Sure,' I said, flicking my ash into the ashtray on the table.

Zelia handed me our passports and gave me a kiss

on the head, then went back inside. 'And Martin, don't forget we only need carry-on luggage,' she yelled from the kitchen.

I took out my phone, a pay-as-you-go I'd bought to replace Martin's. I couldn't keep his old phone; everything on it was triggered by his fingerprint. The night he died I'd accessed his bank account details and the pin numbers to his credit cards via his dead index finger. I'd stored all Martin's contacts in the new phone and then sent out a general text to say this was his new number. I knew he'd said he'd cut any ties with his past, but I couldn't risk a great-aunt or old school pal reaching out to him out of the blue. I had to cover every eventuality, and a quick response to say I was fine would be better than no response at all.

I typed in 'cheap flights to Rome from Paris' and waited for it to load. As I did, I peered down at Zelia's passport photo. She looked young, early twenties at a push. I then noticed the expiry date. It had expired six months ago.

'Zelia, your passport is out of date!' I shouted.

She stepped out onto the balcony. '*Que je suis bête*! I've given you my old one. I only changed it a few months back. They were both in the bedroom drawer together. Give it here and I'll fetch you the new one.'

I handed her the passport. 'You were cute when you

were younger, babe.'

She slapped me on the head. '*Effrontée!*'

I scrolled through the flights, savouring my wine, the afternoon sun satisfying against my skin. There were hundreds to choice from. Air France, Lufthansa, Ryanair, ITA Airways. Direct, one stop, cheap, expensive. You could fly from Charles de Gaulle, Orly or Beauvais-Tille.

I drained my wine and was ready for another. 'Zelia, I'm going to need some help with this. And bring the wine out, would you, darling?'

Zelia eventually came back outside. I don't know how long she'd had been as I'd nearly drifted off again. I was alerted by her presence when I felt the tantalising heat of the sun leave my skin abruptly. I gently opened my eyes, her lean silhouette slowly coming into focus.

'What's the nearest airport to us, babe?' I said scrambling from my slumped position and picking my phone up out of my lap. But something was wrong.

She looked like she'd seen a ghost. Her face was pale and gaunt, as if all the blood had been syphoned from it.

'What's the matter, darling?'

'The drawer got stuck, so I yanked it open and the drawer below came out and smashed to the ground.' Her voice was nothing but a whisper, her words spaced out, a crippling affliction in her tone.

'That's OK, I'll fix it,' I said nervously, knowing

there would be more.

'I found this.' She held out a passport. Not a French one. A British one.

35

It was the chest of drawers from the old apartment. The drawer that had smashed to the floor was the one holding the secret compartment I'd fitted. The secret compartment holding my real passport.

'I can explain,' I whimpered, sounding as convincing as a politician trying to rectify taxes. I made to get up.

'You fucking stay where you are.' She pulled a kitchen knife from behind her back.

I did as she said, lowering myself back into the chair slowly, my eyes never leaving hers. 'Babe, what are you doing? Let me explain to you.'

She took a step back, glanced down at the passport photo and then back at me. 'This man is *l'éventreur de Londres*!'

I didn't need *Fluent in Three Months* for this one. I'd heard it a hundred times on the news, on the radio, from people at work, people in bars. I'd seen it written in black-and-white across every newspaper, and online.

The London Ripper had become a sensationalised, infamous figure across the whole of Paris.

Zenith Provoski's body had been found two weeks after I killed her. They pinned the murder on the London Ripper, along with that of Alberto Beauséjour. They were right to do so. But there were also other killings. A prostitute left split open and dumped by a canal. A gay couple shot at point-blank range while having sex in their car in a secluded location. The press were having a fucking field day with it. My picture had been all over France for the first few weeks, and just when I thought the hype was finally dying down it would all come flooding back, when a new victim without a suspect was again linked to me. Up until a week ago it had been the longest period without a mention of the Ripper. Then just like that it had reared its ugly head again. A young girl who went by the name of Noémie Delautrette had been abducted, raped and then killed on her way home from a nightclub. There was a media frenzy.

L'Eventreur a Encore Frappé! (The Ripper Strikes Again!) was the headline in *Le Parisien,* which had laid on our kitchen table only a few days ago. They would reinstate the same photo – one that looked like it had been taken from a work pass or something, as I was wearing a shirt and tie. The headlines never bothered me. OK, at first it did, when I first saw my face splashed

264

over the front of every newspaper. However, in time I was so confident with my transformation into Martin Hawker, I couldn't care less how many times another story surfaced and my mug shot and name reappeared all over the country. If anything, the more stories linking me to different murders appeared, the more it showed they were still nowhere nearer to catching the Ripper. It was a tip of the hat towards me, a reassuring reminder of my accomplishment. I thought I was untouchable, an invisible parasite living off the spirit of Martin Hawker. Until now, that was.

'Zelia, please, this is crazy talk.'

'The Ripper is you, Martin, isn't it? Or whatever your fucking name is. The person in this passport is fucking you.'

'Zelia, stop it. My hair is a different colour. My eyes are a different colour.'

'So why do you have his fucking passport? You could have dyed your hair, got contacts for your eyes.'

'Zelia, as if you could possibly think I was behind such terrible things. Take last week, for example. The girl that was killed leaving the nightclub. We were out for dinner that night, remember? We both said we were only a few streets away from the club the night it happened. Zelia, darling, please—'

'So explain why you have his passport?'

'I will, babe, I will. Just put the knife down and relax. It's fucking me, for Christ's sake. The person you love. You know the passport isn't me. If you thought it was me, you'd have left the apartment the moment you saw it. Please put the knife down.'

She gradually started to lower her arm, which trembled furiously.

I tried to think of a reason why I could have the passport. Maybe I'd found it and didn't want to hand it in, just in case they tried to pin the murders on me. But then why would I have taken it and gone to the trouble of hiding it? It wasn't plausible at all. Fucking hell. I couldn't believe I was in this situation. Everything I'd gone through to get to here. I tried to think of something else, anything to give me a bit more time, but time wasn't on my side, and neither, now, was Zelia.

She abruptly raised the knife to my face, a surge of energy, a jolt from her shoulder. It had practically been by her side, her defences lowered, her trust temporarily reinstated. Something had triggered a reaction. Her faith in me had instantaneously disintegrated, as if the half-eaten body of the real Martin Hawker now stood behind me, shadowed by a herd of pigs.

'You know I would never have dreamed it, but looking at you now, especially without your glasses on, it's as clear as day.'

We both glanced towards my glasses on the table. I made to grab them.

'Don't you fucking dare,' Zelia said, waving the knife as close to my face as she could. I leaned back in the chair, hesitantly. She was erratic, out of control, her whole life flipped on its head in a matter of moments. I didn't move an inch, my body frozen. It was like I was watching a dream unfold in front of me.

Zelia picked the glasses up from the table and pushed them over the bridge of her nose.

'The lenses. They're plain glass!' she cried, stumbling back.

36

Zelia scurried into the apartment. She only got as far as the kitchen before I grabbed her by the arm. She turned, screaming hysterically, brandishing the knife towards me and running the blade across my stomach, slashing my skin. I winced, falling back against the wall. I looked down. Blood was seeping through my white shirt. I would live, it was only a slight incision, but it stung like hell. She came for me again, wielding the knife above her head, running towards me like a fucking psychopath.

There was more venom in her demeanour this time as she tried to thrust the blade deep into my chest with both hands. She wasn't lashing out like a second ago; this blow was intended to kill me. As the knife came haring down towards my body I managed to reach out and grab her wrists, stopping the forward motion of her arms. We scuffled for a brief second. She gave it everything she had, with an inner strength, desperately trying to overcome me. She squirmed like a worm on a hook, twisting her body in every direction in an attempt to free herself. It was no good. Slowly but surely I started to take control, squeezing her wrists so hard she eventually dropped the knife.

I flung her around into the wall, wrapped my hands around her neck, and stuck my thumbs hard into her windpipe, just as I had done with Zenith Provoski all those months previous. She struggled, pushing her hands into my face, but I just kept adding more pressure until she eventually collapsed within my grasp.

I will never forgot the look on her face as I squeezed the last bit of life out of her – total disbelief and sorrow.

Death by strangulation was slowly becoming my forte with women.

37

I'd sat next to her body drinking wine for hours before I finally went to the bathroom to check the extent of my flesh wound. It was nothing. As I said, I would live. Unfortunately.

I don't know why I killed her. I should have just let her go and waited for my comeuppance. In the heat of the moment maybe I thought I could get away with it, concoct another plan to save myself and delay my incarceration. But Zelia wasn't like Martin Hawker. She had friends and family all over the city. Why didn't I just let her go? Killing, it had become a fucking habit.

I went back into the kitchen and fixed myself a drink. Vodka, this time, straight. Ignoring her body on the floor, I took my glass and the remaining bottle and stepped out onto the balcony, where I pulled up a chair and sat down at the small, round wrought-iron table.

It was 9:15 pm. The sky was clear, a faint half-moon and a dying sun shared the horizon. I lit a smoke. It was quiet, apart from the occasional car fading into the labyrinth of cobbled streets beneath me.

I drank my drink and I poured another. I finished the whole bottle by 10 pm.

I remember seeing 10:15, nothing more.

38

My eyes flickered open to a darkened room. I was in bed, the sheets were cold.

There was a window with Persian blinds. The blind was pulled down but the slats were tilted, allowing a pale moonlight to squeeze into the room, casting shadows that jutted across the ceiling like horizontal bars, imprisoning me. I panicked. The walls around me seemed to be closing in. Where was I?

I jolted forward, sitting upright, and gasped at the silhouettes of two people sitting in at the end of the bed.

'Don't be alarmed.' The man's voice echoed in the night. He got up and walked towards me. He was the size of a mountain. I pushed myself back, crashing into the steel frame of the bed, nowhere to go. He got closer, right up alongside me. I could smell the smoke on his clothes, the stale coffee on his breath. His chest was wheezy, it rattled with every gulp of air. A fifty-a-day habit sitting on his lungs.

I couldn't move. Who were they? What did they want from me?

A switch was flicked beside the bed. The room suddenly lit up, blinding me.

'That's better.'

My eyes slowly adjusted to the light. I glimpsed up at the ogre of a man towering over me. His head was shaved to the skin; the fluorescent lights bounced off his scalp. His dense, grizzled beard shrouded half his face. I could just make out his beady eyes through thick-rimmed glasses. He must have been in his late fifties and was easily over twenty stone. A walking fucking heart attack.

He made his way back to his seat, a slow shuffle, his back hunched.

I could see the other person clearly now. Another male, more of a boy, straight out of uni. A scrawny specimen of a human being. He was wearing a white lab coat that hung off his body. His face was gaunt and covered in acne, his eyes were sunken under thick, dark bags. His thin, black receding hair was slicked back.

'So how are we doing?' The big guy's voice was incredibly soft for his size. He, too, was wearing a white lab coat, undone over a flannel shirt that gaped between each button. He was holding a clipboard. His fingers were puffy and his nails chewed. He had on a cheap digital watch that pinched his skin.

'Who are you? Where am I?'

'All in good time. We just need to ask you some questions.'

'I'm not telling you shit until you tell me who you are and where I am.'

'I'm afraid it doesn't quite work like that. You give us some answers, then we will give you some answers. I would strongly recommend you comply.'

Seriously, who the hell were these guys? I needed to get out. I scanned the room. There was a door. It was shut, but I made a beeline for it.

What the fuck?

I couldn't move. I looked down. I was chained to the bed.

'There's nowhere to run, my friend. If you don't talk, we have no other option than to make you talk.'

They both stood up and came towards me. I fought hard against the cuffs restraining me. It was useless. I was pinned down like a dead moth on exhibition.

They stood at the foot of the bed, one either side of me. I tried to cry for help but no sound came out. The scrawny kid reached into his coat pocket. If it wasn't for the cuffs I could have snapped him in two. He pulled out a gun and thrust the barrel hard into my temple. Checkmate.

'Now, I'm going to ask you some questions,' said the big man. 'If you don't co-operate. my friend here will put a slug right through your head. I don't particularly want to be washing your brains from the wall, so do we have a deal?'

I nodded.

'Excellent. I knew you'd see sense. So let's begin with your name.'

'Martin Hawker.'

'And where do you live, Martin?'

'Paris.'

'Do you also work in Paris?'

'Yes.'

'Who do you work for?'

'Regnard and Sons.'

'And how long have you lived in Paris?'

'Six months.'

'Do you live alone?'

'No, I live with my girlfriend.'

'And what's her name?'

'Zelia Gayson. Look, I didn't do it, alright?'

'Do what?'

'Kill her. I didn't kill her. I didn't kill her!'

'Dr Broccoli – end this now.'

'As you wish, Dr Saltzman.'

He cocked the revolver and took two steps back, the

barrel bearing down on me, right between my eyes, point blank.

'Please, I beg you, I'm sorry!'

He pulled the trigger.

My head hit the table. A bottle crashed to the ground. I sat upright, a cold sweat caking my body, and gathered my bearings. I was outside, on the balcony. I checked my watch. 3 am. Then I lit a smoke, took a deep lungful and slouched back down into the chair. My arms collapsed by my sides, my eyes slowly shut again. The cigarette rolled out of my fingertips.

39

Saturday morning, 10:40 am. My watch glistened as my eyes opened slowly to a new day, blinded by the sun. The sky was clear. Not a single cloud. A perfect azure blue.

It was already warm. I stood up and was greeted by a sore head. My mouth was bone dry; you could have lit a match against my tongue. I peered around. An ashtray full of butts, and an empty bottle of vodka by my feet. No wonder I felt like shit. I picked a cigarette up off the floor, just a tail of ash. I remembered the dream.

I undid my shirt and slung it on the floor, then moved to the edge of the balcony and stretched my arms. I rested them on the rail and peered down to the street below.

Saturday morning, 10:41 am. The world below was going about its business, a business I was soon to be no part of. I had made up my mind. I knew what I was going to do.

I turned and headed back towards the balcony doors,

but before entering the apartment I glanced round one last time.

It was only two weeks ago that Zelia and I had shared a bottle of champagne – Dom Perignon, the good stuff – and toasted our new lives together, looking out to the very same horizon I was staring at now. It had been a beautiful warm evening. We'd sat out until the early hours, got drunk and fucked on the tiles beneath me. I cherished the moment, bottling it up, then wiped the tears from my face and went inside.

The apartment was hot and sticky. There was little air, if any air at all. Her body lay where I'd left it. In this sort of heat I imagined the decomposing process would speed up quite dramatically. It would be only a matter of time before her cadaver was letting off an odour I didn't want to stick around for. The pungent smell of death, a sickly sweet aroma. Hang around for long enough and you'll be so sick you'll be left wondering if you have any intestines left.

I ignored what I'd done, didn't even stand over her body one last time. Nothing was going to change now, so instead I took a cold shower, got dressed and left the apartment. I shut the door and posted the key back through the letter box. I don't know why I did that. What would it matter if I had my key on me when they asked me to hand over my possessions? But for some strange reason it felt right. Some sort of closure. The end of the road.

I passed Monsieur Truffaut in the hall. He was struggling with his own key in the door as he juggled two heavy shopping bags.

'Let me get that for you, Monsieur Truffaut.'

'*Tu es très gentil.*'

I took his key and let him into his apartment. '*Au revoir*, Monsieur Truffaut.'

'*Au revoir…*' He stumbled over my name.

'Mr Hawker,' I said in a flash.

'Mr Hawker. Why, of course!'

He would be shocked over the next few hours when they came, but by then I wouldn't give a shit. By then I would be dwelling in a holding cell, waiting on some slick detective to grill me.

The *Poste de Police* was three streets from where I lived. I passed it every day on the way to work. I'd left the apartment block a free man, but soon I would be a condemned one.

Every dog has their day, or so they say, and I'd definitely had mine, but this was the end for sure. It was fun while it lasted, but there was too much to cover up now; I'd taken it as far as I could. I was on my last drink in the last chance saloon, the bell had rung twenty minutes ago and the barman was standing over me like

279

the grim reaper. It was time to hit the road.

40

The winding streets of Paris were coated in a glorious golden sunshine. In fact, everything the sun's rays hit looked picturesque, from the spiralling church steeples even to the drains below my feet. The sun did that – made everything alright with the world, made you want to reach for your phone and capture the moment. Even today, even after what I'd done, the sun made me feel good.

I continued west to the *Poste de Police*, taking everything in: the electric blue sky above me; the rich green colour of the trees that lined every street; the sound of birds singing; the smell of freshly baked bread from a bakery nearby; the people I passed young and old, all of whose faces I tried to remember; the feel of the cobbled streets beneath me; the taste of the crisp air flowing through my lungs. Freedom.

It was peculiar how good I actually did feel. Maybe these last moments of freedom I was experiencing tasted like that last meal on death row. Savouring every last bite, memorising each individual flavour, so when they stuck in that lethal injection you were back eating that fried chicken. That's what I was doing – capturing this moment to call upon it when I lay awake at night in a dark damp cell.

By the time I reached Raphaël's It was exactly 12 pm. A church bell rang in the distance.

Raphaël's was en route. The *Poste de Police* was now only one block away. I had no intention of stopping, I just wanted to get this over with. No point prolonging the inevitable. I stood on the other side of the road. Raphaël's, like everything else, looked wonderful in the sunlight. It had its four usual round tables outside, draped in crisp white tablecloths, with a single vase filled with fresh lilac-coloured sweet peas.

Only one of the tables was occupied. A guy sat facing the sun, his head tilted back towards the sky, his legs outstretched, his arms by his side. Held loosely in his left hand was a champagne flute that fizzed salmon pink. By the shape of the bottle resting in the ice bucket I was guessing Laurent Perrier Rosé, the champagne of the in-crowd.

I licked my lips. I could almost taste the bubbles. Fuck it, one last drink. What harm could it do?

I stepped across the road and pulled up a chair at the adjacent table, the screeching of the iron legs against the pavestones alerting the guy to my presence. He sat up, turned and smiled in my direction.

'Good afternoon,' I said.

'Good afternoon,' he replied. American.

Two became three as a waiter joined us, a young lad I'd seen on numerous occasions. He was wearing a black waistcoat and a white shirt as crisp as the tablecloth beneath me. He recognised me too.

'Bonjour. Comme d'habitude, monsieur?'

My usual was a large white wine, a light, crisp and zingy Sauvignon out of the Loire Valley that was very easy on the pallet. However, today was like no other. I wasn't just stopping by on the way home from the office, a sneaky apéritif before dinner. No, this was to be my last drink. Fuck it, let's go out in style.

'Actually, I think I'll have a glass of champagne. Actually, make it a bottle, same as my man here.' I pointed across to the gentleman.

'Of course, *monsieur*. Laurent Perrier Rosé. A fine choice.' He took my menu and went back inside.

'Great minds think alike, eh?' said the guy.

'Indeed they do,' I said, laughing, the in-crowd in full flow.

And then, just like that, it was there again from nowhere. That smell of disinfectant burning away at my lungs.

41

Although he spoke with an American accent he was of Asian descent.

His great-great-grandfather had been one of the first Chinese immigrants to arrive in America for the California gold rush of 1849.

My new-found friend had joined me, literally picked up his ice bucket, plonked it on the table, and sat right next to me. He hadn't shut up. I think he was high. No, come to think of it he was definitely high. Cocaine. I knew the tell-tale signs, one being the urge to chat utter shit.

He was around sixty, I guess. He was wearing small, black, circular-rimmed glasses, like the ones John Lennon used to wear. He had a mushroom haircut. The skin on his face was crêpey, dark, well-lived-in. He was dressed well, in a white linen shirt with the sleeves rolled up, tailored black shorts and sandals.

'I'm rambling, do forgive me,' he said. 'This fizz

goes straight to my head.'

And the rest, I thought.

'Do you live in Paris?' I asked.

'I keep a château in Saint-Germain-en-Laye, on the outskirts of Paris. My wife used to love the wine from the region. My main residence, however, is still in Los Angeles.'

Impressive, I thought. This guy fucking reeked of money. And had he and his wife split up? Had she died? I have to admit I was a little surprised to hear he was married. He had very camp mannerisms. Now, I know that doesn't mean anything, and despite my ever-growing list of unethical qualities I don't usually stereotype. I didn't probe any further into his marriage. The conversation was totally one-sided, anyway, due to my new companion's love of the white powder. I was sure to find out sooner or later.

'I'm a writer. Saint-Germain-en-Laye is great for my brain. I've penned twelve novels from my château. I have an office that looks out onto a beautiful vineyard. It stimulates me, it really does.'

'Sounds perfect.'

'It really is. Between you and me, I'm done with LA, I really am. I'm not going back. Never. Wild horses couldn't drag me there.'

'What about your wife? Does she feel the same?' I

ignored the fact that he'd spoken of her in the past tense.

'My wife is dead. She died a month ago today.'

'I'm so sorry. I didn't mean to intrude.'

'Don't be sorry, my friend. You didn't know. It's OK, anyhow. She's in a better place now. She had cancer, first in the lung, and then it went to her brain. It killed her within six months of being diagnosed. The last three months were hell on earth.'

'I can only imagine.'

He moved to the edge of his seat. He was stick thin, with legs like pipe-cleaners. He crossed one leg over the over, sat up straight and folded his arms. He looked like he needed untying.

'The last weeks of her life she was nothing more than a bag of bones, death practically warmed up. Why, if she'd been a horse they would have shot her. I wanted to get her out long before. Switzerland, assisted suicide, die with some fucking dignity, you know? Die when you knew what time of day it was; die when you still had the ability to stop yourself from shitting the fucking bed.'

'Why didn't you?'

'Her family were having none of it. They were devout Roman Catholics, totally against euthanasia, so instead we just watched the cancer eat away at her. I'm glad I never have to see them again.'

'Why won't you see them again?'

'Jeez, the nuts and bolts of it. I think you're going to need another one of them.' He pointed to my empty glass. I took the champagne bottle from the ice bucket and poured another.

'That's better. Now, at least let me know your name before I let you in on my dark secret.'

I laughed inside. Dark secret. If only he knew who he was talking to.

'Martin,' I said. 'Martin Hawker.'

'Lee Chang.' He stood up to shake my hand. His skin was soft, his palms silky smooth. He hadn't done a hard day's work his whole life. Just like Alfredo. My dear Alfredo, I dread to think what was he going to make of the headlines that were soon to be plastered across every front page. He sat back and took a sip of his drink. I noticed he wasn't wearing a wedding ring. 'Elizabeth and I loved each other very much, but neither of us was in love, if you know what I mean.' (I did.) 'Our marriage was platonic. I think I was in love with her at the start, but the start was a very long time ago. We were childhood sweethearts, got married young. We didn't know who we were, let alone know each other. She came from a wealthy background, and when I eventually became successful we had it all. From the outside it seemed like we had the perfect life together. We were married for forty years, the first two legit, after that not so much.

But neither of us wanted to give up what we had – the house in LA, the château here. Don't get me wrong, if we hadn't got along it would never have worked, but somehow it did. We were more like brother and sister. We lived together, did things together, but never slept together. She preferred rugged men, real action heroes, the type of guy who would chop down a twenty-foot tree and carry it home on his shoulder for firewood. Myself, well, I just preferred men.'

'Did you both know this?'

'Know what?' Chang ran his hand through his mop of thick black hair.

'That you were into men and she was into, well, other guys?'

'Of course, darling. There were many times when I caught a guy leaving her room in the dead of night, and vice versa.'

'I am still a little confused,' I said. 'Why will you never see her family again?'

'I'll never forget how they let Elizabeth die. She didn't have to suffer like that. The cancer didn't just beat her, it fucking destroyed her.'

Tears began to well in Chang's eyes. I reached out and rubbed his arm. He smiled at the gesture and dabbed his eyes with a handkerchief. Was he wearing eyeliner? I think he was, as the crisp white handkerchief was now smeared with black pigment.

'Her funeral was two weeks ago today,' Chang said. 'I jumped on a plane without telling anyone, that very night, and came here. This is home now. A new chapter. I can finally be me, without the pretence. No one knows I'm even here.'

'What about your own friends and family back in LA?'

'My parents are both dead and I'm an only child. I don't have many friends, just acquaintances. Lizzy was the only friend I ever needed. I suppose you could say I am a bit of a recluse. All I need is a good idea for a book and I can shut myself off from the world. Anyway, darling, please, enough about me. What about you? Girlfriend? Wife? Boyfriend? Husband? Single? I'm intrigued, darling, I really am.'

'I'm currently single. Just split up from my boyfriend.'

'Darling, I am sorry to hear that.'

'Don't be. It was a mutual decision.'

'Well, it's his loss, whoever he was.'

I knew given half the chance Chang would fuck me. He was a sixty-odd-year-old homosexual, high on cocaine, and with no place to be. So I made it easy for him.

'So what are your plans, Lee?' I asked. 'For the rest of the day, I mean.'

'Nothing much. Nothing much at all. Another drink here, maybe? What about you?'

'Likewise.'

'No job to go to?'

'Today was the day I moved out of my ex's apartment, so I took the day off.'

'So you're obviously not a Parisian, darling. England, I'm guessing?'

'Yes, London. I relocated out here a few years back with work. I'm staying with a friend until I can find a place of my own. It's a bit cramped, but it will do for the short term.'

'Sounds horrendous, darling. I for one need my own space.'

'I bet you're rattling around in your château.'

'Granted it's big, but it's a quarter of the size of my LA home. Listen, you're at a loose end, I'm at a loose end. Why don't you come and see for yourself? It's only a twenty-minute cab journey away. I have plenty more of this stuff.' He shook the neck of the bottle in the ice bucket. The sound of shuffling ice enticed me. 'We can sit on my balcony,' he went on. 'The views are to die for. And if you get too hot, darling, we can always have a dip in the pool.'

'You have a pool?'

Chang didn't say anything. He just took a sip of his

pink champagne and winked.

'OK, sounds perfect,' I said. 'Let me settle up here and we can get going.'

'Don't be silly, darling, you keep your money for your new apartment. This is on me.' He signalled he wanted the bill, and the waiter arrived moments afterwards with a leather wallet and a card machine.

'Add twenty Euro, please,' Chang said.

'*Merci, monsieur.*' The waiter punched in the total and passed the card machine over. Chang pulled a card from a Hermès wallet. It was a visa debit card, a bank account.

The afternoon sun had risen above the canopy. I was now sitting in the shade. I got up from the table, passed Chang and went out into the direct sunlight.

'Beautiful day,' I said, looking up towards the sky. Then I glanced over my shoulder. I'd timed it just right.

42

I took a gulp of air and inhaled it deep through my lungs. I took it all in, the day around me. The sun was warm. It felt good against my skin as it always did. There wasn't a cloud in the sky. The road hummed with passing traffic. A whining Lambretta, the deep chug of a diesel engine from a passing taxi cab, a Mercedes Benz with the roof down playing loud music, a young couple in dark shades moving to the track in perfect harmony.

An elderly couple dressed for lunch passed right by me. I could smell her rich, sickly perfume as it lingered in the air. They entered the restaurant, arm-in-arm, love's young dream. A slight breeze flicked the tops of the slim trees that lined the street around me, disappearing into the distance, a perpetual line of evergreen. I started to smell the food cooking in Raphaël's kitchen, the zesty aroma of spiced meat, the smoking charcoal from the grill, the waft of burning alcohol. I would recommend the steak to the elderly couple.

The church bell in the distance told us all it was 1 pm. A scattering of birds broke from a nearby rooftop, startled by the chime. A group of schoolkids were buying pastries from the bakery opposite. They laughed and joked as they chased each other in the street. A man strolled by with his dog, a small breed of some sort that could have easily fitted in his pocket. A young mum was pushing her newborn child in between sips of a much-needed coffee.

I took it all in. Freedom.

I turned back at Chang. He was smiling in his seat, looking out to me. Checking me out?

'So what do you say, darling?' he said. 'Finish these last drinks and I can order a taxi cab?'

'Sounds good. I'm just going to use the gents.'

I couldn't believe the good fortune presented to me. It was like meeting Martin Hawker all over again. An improbable coincidence.

Chang, however, would be completely different from Hawker. Martin was for life, an aspiration, an enduring way out, a premeditated change. There would be no longevity if I killed Chang; the trail would be too hot, especially when they found Zelia. But what did I have to lose? If I went back with Chang, killed him and left his body in a cupboard to rot, who knows how long it would take them to find me? I would treat it as a final

293

holiday before a life behind bars, every day a bonus, like a patient with a terminal illness.

I'd only ever need to leave the château to get supplies, the occasional venture out to get fresh food. I'd stock up on everything else – cigarettes, alcohol. I'd hopefully find his drug dealer in his phone, too. Money wouldn't be an issue, I had made out Chang's pin when he paid the bill. The transactions on my card would be monitored for certain.

Then I'd sit and wait, days, weeks, however long it took.

I hoped when they finally came for me they'd find me in the pool, floating on a lilo, sipping a cocktail. I'd be tanned, soaked in oil, designer shades and swimming trunks both courtesy of Chang. They'd burst into the garden, bearing down on me, bullet-proof vests on and semi-automatic firearms raised, ready to kill.

'Freeze! Put your hands where we can see them!' one of them would shout.

'Fellas, what took you so long? Pour yourselves a drink,' I'd respond. It would be a fitting ending for the infamous Ripper. I could see the headlines now:

Ripper Finally Caught in Luxurious Bolt-Hole. He Even Offered Drinks to His Captors!

It would sound a lot better than *Ripper Hands Himself in with His Tail between His Legs.*

If I was going to spend the rest of my life in prison, better to give my fellow inmates an indication that I was a ruthless killer who didn't give a fuck. Then maybe, just maybe, that guy in the shower would think twice before trying to stick it up me.

I walked into Raphaël's, past the elderly couple, who were sitting just outside the front door. They were drinking wine. My nostrils were reminded of her thick scent.

It was too nice a day to be sitting inside, and it was quiet. However, there was a woman sitting at the bar. She had her back to me. She was wearing a thick coat, which was odd. It must have been 30°C outside. There was something familiar about her, but I continued to the toilets, which were at the back of the restaurant, to the left of the bar. I'd catch her face on the way back out.

I took a piss, thinking about how I'd kill Chang. Drown him in the pool, maybe?

I washed my hands and checked myself out in the mirror, before dabbing my face with a paper towel. It was hot today. I thought about the woman in the coat. What was she thinking?

I stepped back outside. She was still at the bar. Her head was down, and I couldn't see her face. She was holding a polystyrene cup; there was steam coming from it. As I grew closer to her I began to feel cold, then feel dizzy. I reached out to steady myself against the bar, but it wasn't there, just thin air. I crashed to the floor.

I don't know how long I was out for, but when I finally came round my vision was blurred. I tried to focus, but all I could see was a brilliant light. My mouth was bone dry, the essence of champagne evaporated from my lips. I tried to check the time, but my watch was gone. I tried to get up, but then someone eased me back down. A silhouette of a woman then rose above me like an angel.

43

That goddammed smell again, disinfectant burning away at the back of my throat. Where was it coming from? I was disoriented, my mind a fucking mess. Was I dreaming?

She was still there, all I could see – a woman, her features disfigured like a Picasso painting. I tried to get up again. Digging my elbows hard into the floor, I arched my back, then put my hands on the floor and pushed with everything I had, until I was sitting up on my arse. The woman backed off, towering above me.

I was surrounded by blinding white walls. I could make out a window. The sky was overcast.

'Can you hear me?'

My vision was improving by the second. I could now make out her face.

I got up from the floor slowly, and she reached out and took my arm. We stood opposite each other, she holding my hands. There was a worried look on her face; she seemed pale and drawn. She wore no make-up. I tried to speak, but the words wouldn't come out.

'Take your time,' she said, her voice soft, reassuring. 'You've had a fall.'

I let go of her hands and went over to the window. We were a few floors up. The courtyard below was dotted with flowerbeds filled with jasmine. There was an old sandstone fountain filled with coins which shimmered beneath the water's surface.

A dying oak hovered over one side of the courtyard, its twisted tree trunk protruding from the concrete slabs. Its black, rotting branches projected long, eerie shadows on the ground below as a beam of sunlight broke between the gaps of dark clouds.

Six wooden benches formed a circle in the middle, strategically placed, facing inwards. In the centre of them was a small weather-beaten bandstand.

I turned back into the room. 'Penny, where the fuck am I?'

44

Penny's long, thick coat covered her whole body like a sleeping-bag. She was drinking tea from a polystyrene cup. She offered me some.

'No, thanks. Penny, what the fuck is going on here?'

She'd moved to stand alongside me at the window. It had started to rain. She put her cup down on the window-shelf and grabbed both my hands.

'I know this is hard for you, but I promise you all will be explained. I need to call someone. Someone who will help you.'

'Help me?' I said angrily. 'I just want to know where I am, how I got here and what the fuck is going on!' I looked around the room, the blinding white walls boxing me in. There was a bed, a small TV, not much else. The place reeked of disinfectant. 'Am I in hospital? What's wrong with me?'

'I promise everything will be explained shortly.' She let go of my hands and pulled her mobile from her coat pocket. There was a business card tucked away in her phone case and she dialled the number frantically.

She made her way across the room, her phone tight to her ear, and sat down on a chair next to the bed. Then she glanced over at me and smiled, saying into the phone, 'It's Penny. I think it's over.' She hung up.

45

The rain was pounding hard at the window, and the sound of thunder rumbled angrily in the distance. I imagined the courtyard, submerged in water, the fountain overflowing, the lanky branches of the oak drooping in the deluge.

I was no longer at the window. I was sitting on the edge of the bed, next to Penny.

'Who did you phone? What did you mean when you said you think it's over? What the fuck is happening to me, Penny?'

'They'll be here soon. You'll get all the answers you need, I promise.'

'Who's fucking they?'

'Us.' He entered the room, an ogre of a man, and had to duck to prevent himself hitting his head against the door-frame. His hair was shaved to the skin, and the fluorescent lights bounced off his scalp. His dense, grizzled beard shrouded half his face. I could just make out his beady eyes through thick-rimmed glasses. He must have been in his late fifties. He was easily over twenty stone. A walking fucking heart attack.

Out of his shadow stepped another man, or more of a boy, straight out of uni. He was a scrawny specimen of a human being, wearing a white lab coat that hung off his body. His face was gaunt and covered in acne, his eyes sunken under thick, dark bags. His thin, black receding hair was slicked back.

They both pulled up a chair.

'How are we doing?' The voice was soft for such a big man. He was also wearing a white lab coat, undone over a flannel shirt that gaped between each button. He was holding a clipboard. His fingers were puffy and his nails chewed. He had on a cheap digital watch that pinched his skin.

'Who are you and where am I? And why are you stopping my wife from telling me anything?'

'Forgive me, but you must realise this is a very complex situation. I needed to speak with you first before anyone else could, including your wife. She's only doing what she's been told to do.'

'OK, so who are you and where am I? I won't ask again.'

'My name is Dr Saltzman, this Dr Broccoli. He's just sitting in to observe. Don't worry, he doesn't bite.'

I wasn't too sure. A guy who resembled a vampire,

who wasn't going to bite? And a doctor? This kid looked like he'd just been pushed out of his mother's cunt!

'Doctors. So I'm in a hospital?'

'Not quite. Look, I need you to answer some questions for me. It won't take long, I promise. Once I've finished you can ask me anything. You have to trust me here.'

I peered across at Penny. I'd almost forgotten she was there.

'It's for your own good,' she said, clasping her hands together.

I looked back towards Saltzman. 'OK.'

46

'Does the name Martin Hawker mean anything to you?'

'Never heard it before.'

'Are you sure?'

'Yes, I'm sure. Who the fuck is Martin Hawker?'

'All in good time. Have you been to Paris any time in the last six months?'

'No.'

'What's the last thing you can remember before today?'

I had to think. Think hard. I could almost feel the blood rushing to my head to help my brain. I then remembered the lights arriving through the fog.

'I was waiting for a train. I was going to work.'

'Nothing else after that? I really need you to think. It's important.'

'No, nothing.'

'So between waiting for your train and now you don't believe you've been anywhere else?'

'How many more times? I was waiting for a train. Next thing I know I'm in here, wherever here fucking is. Have I been in an accident?'

'I promised you I'd answer any of your questions after I've finished. It's imperative for your wellbeing that I continue this without any further interruptions. Do I make myself clear?'

I nodded reluctantly.

'Have you ever heard of a company called Regnard and Sons?'

'No.'

'Does the name Zelia Gayson mean anything to you?'

'Never heard of it.'

'Are you sure?'

'Yes, I'm fucking sure. What the fuck is all this about? Have I lived in Paris? Random fucking names I've never heard of before?'

'I know this is confusing for you. I only have a few more questions.' He looked across at the gawky kid and raised his eyebrows. Maybe I'd nearly passed their test. If it was a test? I was getting irate. I wanted answers and all I was doing was giving them.

Saltzman focused his attention back on me and crossed his legs, knocking the pen in his hand between his teeth, irritatingly.

'Well?' I said. My tone must have convinced everyone

in the room my patience was running thin.

Saltzman took the pen from his mouth and leaned forward looking deep into my eyes. 'What is your full name? Where do you work? Where do you live and who is this woman in relation to you?'

He pointed at Penny as if I didn't know she was there.

'I told him my name. I then said, 'I work for a data communications company called Zoca. I live in a town called Huntingworth, in Essex. That woman you point to is my wife. Do you want my waist size as well? Star sign?'

Saltzman turned to face Broccoli. The kid was chewing gum with yellow, stumpy teeth. He'd been forever making notes on a clipboard the same as Saltzman's. He glanced up, firstly at me and then across at his superior. He nodded.

Saltzman then continued, 'You've been here with us for the past three months. None of that you recollect. That day you remember, waiting for the train, that was exactly three months ago today. January 27th, to be precise. From what we know you boarded the train and fell asleep. I believe that's when it started.' He looked down at his clipboard and ran his finger across his notes, his eyes squinting like a mole. 'Ah, here we are. We have a Mrs Kitzmiller, a very helpful lady who was on the train with you that very morning. She said you approached her on the platform. She was looking for her ticket and you helped her to find it, which you did. However, when you got to the gates you got into an argument with a guard who you believed wasn't going to let Mrs Kitzmiller through. You then produced a knife. You had to be detained by several staff members who called the police. Do you recollect any of these events?'

'No. No, I don't. What the hell are you talking about?'

'These events happened, that's a fact, but I believe this was the start of your episode. A trigger point. Although you did act out everything I've mentioned, I don't believe you realised what you were doing. I have a theory on this. It's not medically proven, but it's something I believe in.'

'What are you talking about? What do you mean by episode?'

'There was a point in time on that morning, on that train journey, that you slipped into a sort of semi-consciousness. A semi-episode, I like to call it, but again, this is just my theory. However, after drawing a knife, this is when you slipped into a full episode.'

'That fucking word again. Episode! Semi-episode, full episode… What is a fucking episode?'

'A psychotic episode.'

'What the hell? This is bollocks, all of it. Utter bollocks.'

'I need you to be calm. I know this is a lot for you to take in.'

'You're damn right it is. Penny, please tell these guys they don't know what they're talking about. I've been in some sort of accident. That's why I'm here, right? In hospital? Go on, Penny, tell them.'

Penny didn't get a chance to speak. Saltzman intervened in a flash. 'You're not in a normal hospital. This is a psychiatric hospital.'

'What? A fucking nuthouse?'

'We choose not to use those words. A psychotic episode can happen to anyone. It can be caused by alcohol and drug misuse. We know about the pressures you've been under. The cancer. Your debt.'

I looked across at Penny in disbelief. Surely this wasn't happening. Any second now I'd wake up and find myself sitting on the train. Another shit Monday, nothing else. But I didn't wake up. I stayed in the room, the blinding white walls caving in on me. Penny must have found out about the debt, gone through my phone. My heart suddenly sank. Ursula.

Saltzman continued, oblivious to my disquiet. 'A couple of days ago we asked you some simple questions. Your name, where you live, where you work. We were seeing where you were within the episode. A person having a psychotic episode is best left alone. They lose touch with reality; they perceive or interpret reality in a very different way from people around them. It can be dangerous to intervene. We mustn't confront or challenge someone's beliefs. By the book, we should have let you come out of the episode in your own time. However, you showed signs of recognising your surroundings, so I tested you. I asked your name, you said you were Martin Hawker. I asked where you lived, you said Paris. I asked where you worked, you mentioned a company called Regnard and Sons. I asked if you were married. You said no, but you had a girlfriend who went by the name of Zelia Gayson, with whom you lived with. After that you kept screaming that you didn't kill her. We obviously knew then you were still very much within the episode. So all we could do was wait. That day came today, much quicker than we anticipated. When you fell leaving the toilet, that was the first time in three months you recognised who Penny was. Maybe the bump on the head brought you back to us, but in the medical world we're still not one hundred per cent sure what brings someone out of a psychotic episode.'

'So for the past three months you've just been watching me live out this fucking out-of-body experience? I've lost the last three months of my life, no memories, nothing. Tell me what you saw. Where have I been? What did I do?' My throat was dry and full of emotion. I found it hard to speak.

'We'll never fully know what you experienced. We, from the outside, can only get snippets of what's going on inside your head. You were part of another world, a world only you encountered. It's rare for someone in a deep episode to remember everything that happened. Occasionally you may get flashbacks. However, for your own sake I hope you don't. A psychotic episode is usually anything but a happy memory. We need to keep you with us, in this world.'

The room went quiet as I took it all in.

Saltzman got up, and Broccoli followed.

'It's been a lot to take in,' Saltzman said. 'I think we've done enough today. The good news is you're finally back with us. Have some time with your wife. I'll come and see you again tomorrow. Hopefully we can have you out of here within a few days.' He looked over to Penny. 'We'll give you some time alone. Keep talking, it's good for him. I'll have someone come by in a couple of hours.'

They left the room, the man mountain and his willowy shadow.

'A lot to take in,' Penny said. She came over to the bed, sat next to me and took my hand. Did she know about Ursula? If she did, she was playing it pretty cool. Maybe I had all that to come. Get him better, get him home, then rip into the cunt for destroying everything.

I would have done everyone a favour that morning if I'd just jumped. Problem eliminated, crushed beneath the steel wheels of that passing InterCity. Penny could finally move on, be with someone she deserved, someone who would worship the ground she walked on. Not me, not that egocentric parasite who needed to be obliterated.

I wished I hadn't woken from it, whatever it was. It had to be better than here? Wasn't it?

'Are you hungry?' Penny said, rubbing my hand affectionately. 'There's a restaurant downstairs. I can go and get you a sandwich or something?'

I was hungry. Famished, in fact. 'I'll go. I could do with stretching my legs.'

'OK, well let's both go.'

'Penny, do you mind if I go on my own? I could do with five minutes to myself, take it all in.'

'Are you sure you'll be OK?'

'I'll be fine. Just need a little time, that's all. Where is this restaurant?'

'Out of the room, turn right. Take the lift at the bottom of the corridor to the ground floor. Restaurant will be facing you when you come out. Here, put this on.' She passed me a dressing-gown that was hooked on the back of the door.

'Thanks.' I put it on and gave her a kiss on the cheek.

'Back soon.'

I made for the door, but Penny called me back. 'You won't get very far without any money. Unfortunately, it's not all inclusive here.' She took a note from her purse and put it into the pocket of my dressing-gown. She looked me in the eyes. 'You used to call it Raphaël's,' she said.

'Call what Raphaël's?'

'The restaurant here in the hospital. Sometimes you would refer to it as Raphaël's.'

I smiled, then kissed her on the cheek and left the room.

47

The lift descended, the whining of the cables all around me. My head was fuzzy. No real thoughts. An abyss of bewilderment.

The doors pinged open on the ground floor. The restaurant was right there, just as Penny had described. I made my way across the corridor and through the entrance. It was pretty empty. I didn't know what time of day it was. I pulled out a note from my pocket and unfolded it. Fifty Euros. I couldn't recall placing it there.

I went to the bar and ordered two brandies. I asked for the good stuff, twenty-five Euro a shot.

I took my drinks and made my way outside the restaurant. The weather was still fine. A sizzling sun and cloudless sky.

I sauntered past the elderly couple. They were tucking into steak. I was glad they went for it.

'Darling, what you got there?' Chang said, as I sat back down at the table.

'One for the road.' I passed him a glass.

'Why, thank you, darling. I've ordered a taxi. It will be here in ten minutes.'

'Great,' I said, savouring the sting of Hennessy on my lips.

Chang pulled out a box of cigarettes and held them out in front of me.

'Smoke?'

I pulled one from the box. 'Sure. Everyone smokes in Paris.'

The End

Printed in Great Britain
by Amazon